Choke

Choke

Diana López

SCHOLASTIC PRESS / NEW YORK

Library of Congress Cataloging-in-Publication Data Available

ISBN 978-0-545-41822-5

Text copyright © 2012 by Diana López
All rights reserved. Published by Scholastic Press, an imprint of Scholastic Inc., *Publishers since 1920.* SCHOLASTIC, SCHOLASTIC PRESS, and associated logos are trademarks and/or registered trademarks of Scholastic Inc.

10 9 8 7 6 5 4 3 2 1   12 13 14 15 16

Printed in the U.S.A.   23
First edition, July 2012

For my brothers, Albert and Steven

knockout game, airplaning,

rocket ride, sleeper hold,

pass-out game, wall hit,

cloud nine, gasp,

American dream game,

necktie challenge, blackout game,

trip to heaven, flatliner,

hyperventilating,

suffocation roulette

choke

CHAPTER 1

Knockout Game

My middle school has the "in-crowd," the "out-crowd," and the "GP." "GP" stands for "general public," just like the movie rating. The in-crowd works hard to stay out of the GP, while the out-crowd works hard to get in.

I'm definitely GP, general public in every way. When the students line up by height for our class portrait, I stand in the middle row. When I try out for spots on the basketball team and chess club, I get the "alternate" position. When my teachers grade tests, I make B's, sometimes C's, but never F's or A's. I wear glasses, which is a drag, but I don't have pimples, which is cool. I never come in first when we run laps in P.E., but I never come in last, either.

Sometimes I like being GP because no one expects me to run for student council or compete in the academic decathlon. Being GP means being invisible, which is cool when the teachers forget to ask for my opinion, which is *double* cool since I don't have an opinion most of the time, at least not one they would care about. Honestly, I don't know how I feel about the president or YouTube or *The Giver*, a book we had to read in English class. So being invisible has its benefits, but it can be boring, too. Especially around cute guys like Ronnie Esparza. Don't get me wrong. I'm not *completely* invisible around him. We talk — almost every day — but we never have *real* conversations. He'll say, "Hi, Windy" or "Can I borrow a pencil?" but never "Who do you think's going to win the Super Bowl?" or "Will you be my date for the Valentine's dance?" Now those are questions I could answer, questions I *want* to answer. I should ask him first, about sports or for a date, but I'm not brave enough — even though I was the only eighth-grade girl who didn't scream on the roller coasters at Fiesta Texas.

So at the end of the day, being GP isn't good enough. I want to be part of the in-crowd. I want the keys to their golden lockers, the ones that get decorated with streamers and ribbons on Spirit Day. The ones with mirrors on the inside door, mirrors reflecting beautiful faces and surrounded by pictures of beautiful BFFs. Lockers with secret admirer love notes crammed into the air vents. Lockers with wallpaper and vanilla-scented air fresheners. Lockers that have been interior designed, the ultimate sign of an in-crowd girl.

Unfortunately, moving up the social ranks isn't easy. Like I said, I make B's and C's, never A's. I wish I looked like my mom, who is beautiful — *everyone* says so. But I don't. I look like my dad. No one ever calls him ugly, but no one calls him handsome, either. He's normal-looking, and I'm just as normal-looking — from the elastic bands that hold back my hair to my Nike tennis shoes. And even though my parents make decent money, I wear a zirconia ring, not a diamond, and I shop at Target, not Macy's. Without brains, looks, or cash, I had no way of joining the in-crowd. No way at all. At least, not until the day we got back from Spring Break, the day that Nina showed up.

I met her in speech class. No, I met her before I even *saw* her. I met her when my best friend, Elena, said, "Hey, Windy, there's a new girl in school."

That's when I said, "What's she like?"

"She's mag-tastic," Elena said.

She loves combining words like "magnificent" and "fantastic." She calls it "word-morphing," something she's been doing since elementary school. I keep waiting for her to out-grow it, but Elena likes to hold on to things — not just habits like word-morphing but *actual* things like the gym bag, piccolo case, backpack, purse, and lunch box she carries around all day. She holds on to out-of-style fads, too — rubber bracelets with hopeful adjectives stamped on them, socks with pom-poms, and pumpkin or Christmas tree ear-rings that she keeps wearing even when bunny rabbits would be more appropriate. I often tell her to get with the fashion program, to update, but she just points to herself and says, "This is me, take it or leave it." She honestly doesn't care what other people think.

She went on about Nina, "You know how the guys in band always hog up the percussion and brass? How they pick on girls if we even *think* about playing 'their' stuff?"

"Yeah. What does that have to do with the new girl?"

"She walked into band and straightaway told Mr. Hamilton she was a drummer. Of course, the guys started teasing her. They said it takes biceps to play the drums. She flexed her muscles, and the guys started calling her Popeye. So she went up to the lead drummer, pulled two drumsticks from her back pocket, and did a riff. She was better than *all* of them, and to cap it off, she bopped the lead drummer on his head."

"No way," I said, laughing at the image.

Just then, one of the guys did the check-out-that-babe whistle. Everyone looked toward the door where a pretty girl stood with a yellow registration slip in her hand.

"That's her," Elena whispered.

The guy whistled again. Nina didn't blush or hide. She scanned the room, found him, and looked straight in his eyes, a tense stare-down. After a while, the guy looked away. I was impressed. I'd never met a girl who could make a guy slink off like a shamed dog.

At the same time, I couldn't blame him for whistling. Nina was tall, like a model. She had a dark complexion that made her hazel eyes stand out, *real* hazel eyes, not the contact lens kind. She could wear her hair loose because it looked like it belonged on a Pantene commercial — not frizzy and tangled like mine. That day, Nina wore jeans, a blue knit top, and a beautiful scarf with a swirly pattern in blue, purple, and silver. She had tied it around her neck, knotted at the side so the ends draped behind and in front of her shoulder.

"What a knockout," the guy behind me whispered.

The tardy bell rang, so we scrambled to our seats. Mrs. Campos stepped in, took the new girl's registration form, and said, "Hello, class. We have a new student today. Nina Díaz. Please welcome her."

"Hello, Nina Díaz," we all said. Mrs. Campos loved to hear a chorus.

"You'll have to sit by Ronnie," Mrs. Campos told Nina. "I like my students in alphabetical order. That way, I can take attendance in two seconds."

"Where's Ronnie?" Nina said.

He raised his hand, too eagerly I thought. She went to his row, and everyone who came after Nina in the alphabet had to scoot one seat over.

"Quick," I whispered to Elena, taking out my TOP FIVE spiral. "Let's list the top five reasons the new girl's lucky."

"She plays the drums," Elena said. "And she's got great hair."

I wrote them down. "Number three — she's new so she gets a fresh start."

"Don't forget her pretty eyes."

"And the number one reason she's lucky?" I asked. Elena and I looked at each other and at the same time said, "She gets to sit next to Ronnie."

Suddenly Mrs. Campos knocked on the chalkboard. She was staring right at us, and since she'd already threatened to move us for talking too much, Elena quickly turned around. In fact, we always sit next to each other, and we always talk too much. It's not our fault. Blame our teachers because

Elena's last name is Sheppard and mine is Soto. We were bound to become best friends after so many years of sitting in alphabetical order. Sometimes there'd be a Silverton or Smith between us, but not often. I was surprised we still sat together in Mrs. Campos's class. Our math teacher had moved us apart months ago.

After spending thirty minutes lecturing about something called "process analysis," Mrs. Campos introduced our next speech presentation.

"This time, we're not going to do PowerPoints or read from note cards," she said.

"But I hate impromptu speeches," someone complained.

"Don't worry. We're finished with our impromptu speech unit."

"Don't tell us we have to memorize a poem again," another student said.

"No, we're not going to do another poetry recitation." The class waited expectantly, and when Mrs. Campos felt sure no one else would interrupt, she went on. "We're going to use props this time. We're going to do a process analysis by *modeling* something."

"Really?" Alicia, one of the in-crowd girls, nearly jumped out of her chair. "I *love* to model. Can I model my sister's prom dress?"

"That's not what I mean by 'model,'" Mrs. Campos explained. "I mean demonstrate. You're going to do a demonstration."

Alicia's shoulders slumped.

"Too bad for Alicia," I whispered to Elena.

"Yeah. My heart bleeds for her," she whispered back.

We couldn't help "feeling sorry" for Alicia because she and her best friend, Courtney, like to wave their in-crowd status in our faces — every chance they get.

Sometimes I can't believe they used to be our friends. In elementary school, we were Girl Scouts. All four of us loved it, but for some reason, Alicia and Courtney started to keep score. Who sold the most cookies? Who earned the most patches? Elena was the best Girl Scout on the planet, and they hated her for it. So they quit, and because they made jokes about Girl Scouts, Elena and I quit, too, even though we really liked it. Added to that was Elena's star student status. She busted the curve in classes where teachers ranked their students. She was mentioned on the morning announcements and school newsletter more often than a starlet in the tabloids. Alicia and Courtney didn't put as much effort into school, but they still kept score, and every time Elena "beat" them, they made our lives miserable.

We didn't get it. How could two girls who were prettier and more popular be so jealous?

Three years ago, we started middle school at Horace Mann. The school is surrounded by beautiful historical homes, the kind that have maids and gardeners. The regular houses are across Lake Street, and farther down, across Zarzamora, the houses are run-down. I live between Lake and Zarzamora, of course, but Courtney and Alicia live on the historical side, on a street called Kings Highway — and, like royalty, they wore "crowns," headbands with fake gems. Plus, Courtney has blond hair. She's always had blond hair, but now Alicia has it, too. We live in a part of San Antonio where the billboards are in English *and* Spanish. Our neighborhood has a few blonds, but most people here have brown hair. Of course, everyone wanted to copy Courtney and Alicia, including Elena and me. My hair is brown like a chocolate bar. Elena's is somewhere between brown and gold. So we begged our moms to let us bleach our hair. They said no. They said we were beautiful just the way we were. How ridiculous is that? So then I tried to wear pretty head-bands, like all the other girls, but a headband on top of glasses gave me a giant headache behind the ears. I have no hope, no hope at all. I'll *never* look like an in-crowd girl.

"Next year you'll be in high school," Mrs. Campos went on. "So you have to start thinking about where to go, which classes to take. It's not too early to start planning a career. Studies show that attending a magnet school increases your chance of succeeding in college."

Magnet schools were for students who had their goals figured out. Our district had several: for health careers, for business, for fine arts, for science and technology. But me? I wanted to go to a regular school.

"So let's talk about some possible careers," Mrs. Campos suggested.

Alicia raised her hand. "Modeling's a career, isn't it? So I can still model my sister's prom dress, right?"

"That's fine with me," Mrs. Campos said.

"And I want to be a celebrity hairstylist," Courtney added. "Can I partner up with Alicia and fix her hair after she models the dress?"

"As long as you explain the process."

"Trainer," Ronnie blurted.

"What's that?" Mrs. Campos asked.

"I'm going to be the guy who works at a gym and shows dudes how to exercise. They could get hurt if they do it wrong. Pull a muscle maybe. Or the barbell could land on their chest and, like, break their lungs."

"Oh, Ronnie," Courtney said, full of fake sweetness. "Can I be your trainee?"

He nodded, too eagerly, I thought again.

"Anyone else interested in an athletic career?" Mrs. Campos asked.

Elena's hand went up.

"Don't answer," I whispered. "Please don't answer." I knew what she was going to say. I knew she'd embarrass herself. But instead of putting down her hand, she waved it like someone lost at sea.

"Elena," Mrs. Campos said, "what would *you* like to be?"

"A professional ice-skater," she announced.

The whole class cracked up.

"Don't laugh," she said. "This is America. I can be anything I want."

Courtney said, "Do you *really* want to wear leotards?"

The class laughed even louder, and it wasn't because of Elena's weight, because she's not fat. Not really. She just hasn't experienced a growth spurt yet, hasn't stretched out. Like I said, Elena holds on to things, and one of those things is baby fat.

"Besides," Courtney added, "this is San Antonio. It's not like we get white winters here."

"All I need is an ice-skating rink, not an entire frozen lake."

Courtney made a *W* by holding three fingers to her forehead. Everyone knew what it meant. It was the in-crowd sign for "whatever."

"Yeah. Whatever," Alicia added with her own *W* sign.

"You two can be so rude-ocious," Elena said.

"That's not even a word."

"Okay, now," Mrs. Campos warned. "Let's get back to our discussion. But first, Elena, I think it's wonderful to have an aspiring ice-skater in our class. And I wish you the best of luck with your dream."

"She's sure going to need it," Alicia said.

The class laughed again till Mrs. Campos put up her fist. "That's enough!" she said as she counted with her fingers — one, two, three. We knew there'd be detention if she reached five before we hushed, so we quickly settled down. Mrs. Campos held the silence a little longer, and then she turned to me. "Windy, what do you want to be when you grow up?"

I shrugged. "I don't know."

"Well, what are your interests?"

"I don't have any," I said.

"None at all?"

"I just want a job that won't make my feet hurt."

The class chuckled.

"I'm not trying to be sarcastic," I quickly told Mrs. Campos. "I just want a job that lets me sit down all day, so I won't be tired when I get home."

"Maybe you can research office jobs," Mrs. Campos suggested.

I nodded and wrote "office jobs" in my notebook.

Just then, the dismissal bell rang. "Enjoy your lunch," Mrs. Campos said as we filed out. I picked up my things and headed to the door, and as I passed Nina's desk, I realized she hadn't spoken at all. I left the class wondering what she'd like to be, which magnet school she'd apply to. Maybe I could apply there, too.

CHAPTER 2

Airplaning

*I*n the cafeteria, seats are determined by status. The in-crowd sits by the windows overlooking the courtyard. The out-crowd sits by the trash cans and the big plastic vat where we dump our milk before pitching the cartons into the recycling bin. The milk sours fast, so the whole corner stinks, and since it's close to the exit, it buzzes with flies.

The GP sits everywhere else.

Our cafeteria has a serving area with two lines, hot and cold. The cold line offers soggy sandwiches wrapped in cellophane, a variety of chips, apples or oranges, and milk or water. The hot line offers a different menu each day, usually a meat, a vegetable, a fruit, and milk or water. If we want soda or Gatorade, we have to go to the vending machines and spend an extra dollar.

Elena and I prefer the hot line, especially when it features lasagna, which was on the menu on Nina's first day.

"Check out Ronnie," Elena said, nodding toward the vending machines. "He's getting a Dr Pepper, Doritos, and a Snickers bar."

"I thought he wanted to be a trainer," I said. "You can't be a trainer if you're a junk food junkie."

"He's guilty of junk-luttony, that's for sure."

"Not another new word," I pretended to complain.

"Yeah. Junk plus gluttony. Get it?"

"Let's just call him a junkie jock," I suggested.

"Junkie jock versus junk-luttony . . ."

While Elena thought about it, Nina stepped in line behind us. The guys nearby were checking her out, but she didn't seem to notice. She must be used to the school yard paparazzi.

"Hi," she said to me, extending her hand. "I'm Nina."

"Yeah, I know," I said, offering my hand in return. "I'm Windy. I'm in your speech class."

"Office jobs, right?"

"Yeah."

She looked at Elena. "And you're Elena, the ice-skater."

"That's right."

I couldn't believe she remembered us. Like I said, being GP usually makes us invisible.

As I wondered how to keep the conversation going, Alicia and Courtney cut in front of us. I could smell their tangerine lip gloss, vanilla-scented body lotion, and coconut-infused conditioner. They both had Coach purses, identical except for the big, brass initials of their names.

"Excusez-moi," they said, nudging us aside to get their trays.

"That's not fair," Elena said.

"That's not fair," Alicia repeated in a baby voice.

"But we were here first."

This time Alicia and Courtney didn't bother to say "whatever." They simply flashed the *W* sign.

"What's up with them?" Nina whispered.

Elena and I shrugged. We honestly didn't know why Courtney and Alicia picked on us, but we had our theories. Elena said they were jealous. Maybe they were. After all, Elena gets lots of school awards. But I never get any, so why give *me* a hard time? Besides, Courtney and Alicia get their own recognitions — in the yearbook, they were Best Dressed, Most Popular, and Most Likely to Land a Spot on a Reality TV Show. Those are the awards that matter, that will be remembered at reunions ten years from now. No, they weren't jealous. If they were, they'd pick on the other successful GP, too. I think they can read our minds and know we want to be part of the in-crowd. They probably think we don't remember our proper place, so they act mean to remind us.

"Hey, Miss," Courtney said to the cafeteria lady, "make sure you give my little friend here some applesauce since it's the closest thing you have to baby food."

"Maybe you could warm up some milk for her, too," Alicia added.

Elena's face got red, but she didn't have a comeback. Neither did I. Neither did Nina, who seemed to be studying Courtney. Something in Nina's eyes, maybe because they were hazel, reminded me of a cat watching birds at a feeder.

The line had been moving steadily, but Courtney and Alicia, with all their questions, had really slowed it down.

"Do you have a low-carb version of lasagna?" they asked.

"Can we have whole wheat toast instead of French bread?"

"Why do you call this 'salad' when it's just lettuce? Shouldn't salads have lots of different veggies?"

"Yeah, different veggies. And where's the low-fat dressing?"

Finally, they filled two glasses with ice water, paid the cashier, and left the serving area. Meanwhile, the line had backed up, so the people behind us started complaining.

"We don't have all day," we heard.

"Hey, don't give *us* a hard time," I said. "We weren't the ones acting like this is a five-star restaurant."

"Oh, shoot!" Elena shook her head. "I really wanted some applesauce, but I don't want to give Courtney and Alicia the satisfaction."

"Here," Nina said, "I'll put it on my tray, and when we get to the table, I'll pass it to you."

"Really, you'd do that?"

"Sure. What are friends for?"

Elena and I were speechless. We'd never had an in-crowd-worthy friend before.

We finally got through the line, but just as we left the serving area, my foot slipped on something. I quickly lost my balance, so I released my tray and tried grabbing Elena to catch myself, but her foot hit something slippery, too. Ice cubes! A whole bunch of ice cubes! I fell back and got that queasy feeling — like when I used to play airplane by propelling myself off the swings. Only, when I played airplane, I was in control, I was graceful, I was having fun. But here, in the cafeteria, my legs and arms were totally flailing, and as much as I tried to land as gracefully as a cat, I couldn't help landing on my butt. Yes, smack down on my butt, which got wet from the ice cubes, which meant that people would think I peed. Elena and I also had cheese and pasta all over our clothes. Tomato sauce got on my glasses, too, and when I tried to wipe it off, it smudged. To make things worse, Ronnie stood nearby. I was too embarrassed to glance up at him, but I knew it was Ronnie because he was the only one who wore lime green Nikes. This had to be the most humiliating moment of my life. Everyone was having a laugh riot.

"Did you throw this ice on the floor?" Elena asked Courtney.

She took a while to answer because she was giggling so much. "Just wanted to see if you could ice-skate," she said.

This got people laughing even harder, and even though she was a victim, too, I was angry with Elena. I had *begged* her not to tell the class about her odd career choice. Honestly, Elena couldn't even in-line skate, so I *knew* she'd humiliate us somehow. And this wasn't the first time, either. Last semester, while everyone else made volcanoes and terrariums for science projects, Elena crash tested eggs in various landing capsules. She had one with a parachute, one with a bouncy framework of straws, and one with lots of cushioning. She painted scared faces on the eggs, and named them

Snap, Crackle, and Pop. Only Snap survived the drop from the second-floor window.

Okay, I admit that she had a cool project. Double cool since the teacher gushed with pride and gave her the highest score in class. But that was the problem. Being double cool in science meant being double nerdy everywhere else.

That's why Elena had one foot in the out-crowd, and the last thing I wanted was to go down with her.

Thank goodness, Nina didn't think the prank was funny. She walked right up to Courtney and Alicia, invading their precious personal space. She looked down on them because she was so much taller.

"Why don't you go fix your makeup or something?" Nina said.

"Makeup" had never sounded like a bad word before, but it did right then.

"Catfight!" someone called, and a few extra people gathered around.

"If that's what she wants," Nina said, looking directly at Courtney, challenging the leader of the eighth-grade in-crowd.

Courtney glanced at the expectant eyes around her. She wasn't a catfight kind of girl, so she answered with her *W* sign and mouthed the word, "Whatever."

"What's that?" Nina said, cupping her ear. "I didn't hear you."

No one had ever stood up to Courtney. She swallowed hard. She seemed nervous but reluctant to back away.

"Come on," Alicia said, tugging Courtney's sleeve. "We've already wasted too much time on these losers."

The two walked off. Most of the gawkers left, too, but not Ronnie. I finally glanced up. Thankfully, he wasn't laughing. Was he being compassionate and kind, or was his mouth too full of Doritos? A few girls stood around, too. They had laughed earlier, but now they looked totally confused as they glanced at Nina, then Courtney, then Nina again.

Finally, Liz, one of the in-crowd girls, asked if we were okay. Elena and I nodded.

"All right, then," Liz said. "We better get going." She and the in-crowd girls with her hurried to catch up with Courtney, but before they got too far, Liz turned around to wave goodbye. I started to raise my hand, but she wasn't saying bye to me. She was saying bye to *Nina*.

"See you later," Nina called. When the girls finally reached their seats at the far end of the cafeteria, Nina said, "Hey, Ronnie. Come help us, will you?"

Like us, he seemed surprised that she remembered him.

"Sure thing," he said.

He picked up my tray, his fingers still orange from Doritos. I didn't know whether to feel grateful or mortified. Like I said, we talked every day, but that was because Ronnie was nice to *everyone*. Not because he *liked* me or anything.

"You sure you're all right?" he asked.

"I'll recover."

"I know. You're a real trouper," he said.

He might have winked at me, or maybe he had some dust in his eye. In any case, he didn't say anything else, just picked up our trays and walked off.

"Thanks for sticking up for us," Elena said as Nina gave us a wad of paper towels so we could wipe the cheese and pasta from our shirts.

"Yeah. Thanks," I said.

"No problem," Nina told us. "Every school has mean girls like that. If you let them get to you, they just act worse. Eventually, someone will put them in their place. Trust me." She helped us up. "Besides," she added, "those girls don't know the meaning of breath sisters."

Elena and I glanced at each other. We didn't know the meaning, either, but we weren't about to admit it.

CHAPTER 3

Rocket Ride

*E*lena came to my house after school. I'm a latchkey kid, which is a good thing when you have tomato sauce all over your clothes.

"So what do you think 'breath sister' means?" Elena asked as we turned onto my street.

"I have no idea, but I'm sure it's something cool."

We got to my house, and just as I put my key in the door, we heard meowing in the nearby bushes. We went to investigate, and as I pushed aside some branches, a beige kitten scrambled to hide.

"Hello, there," I said. "Where's your mommy?" The kitten stared at me and blinked. "Keep an eye on it," I told Elena. "I'm going to get some food."

"But shouldn't . . ."

Before she could finish her sentence, I rushed into the house.

Sunny, my orange cat, and Cloudy, my gray cat, ran figure eights around my legs, while El Niño, my black cat with a white, lightning-shaped mark on its forehead, lounged on the windowsill. Even though *niño* means "boy" in Spanish, the name has nothing to do with my cat's gender. Instead it refers to a warm water current that causes crazy weather patterns. My dad is a meteorologist, so you can guess who named them all (and where *my* name came from).

"I'll feed you guys in a minute," I promised as I grabbed a bowl, whipped an egg, and returned outside.

"Don't," Elena warned.

I ignored her. "Here, kitty, kitty," I called.

The kitten peeked out. I set down the bowl and slowly stepped away. As soon as the kitten felt safe, it tiptoed out, sniffed the bowl, and lapped up the egg.

"How can I ignore the big blue eyes of a hungry kitten?" I asked Elena.

"You made a cross-my-heart-hope-to-die promise about leaving stray cats alone. I was there, remember? Your mom made me a witness. You're going to get in a whole lot of trouble if you do this."

26

"Maybe, but like you always say, sometimes you have to riskify."

We watched the kitten for a little while, and then we went inside. Sunny, El Niño, and Cloudy meowed as I prepared their food.

"I'm going to your room to put on a clean shirt," Elena said. Luckily, she had left an extra shirt at my house the week before.

"Bring one for me, too."

I put the cat food in three separate bowls, since they'd rather fight than share. Then I sat beside them and scratched behind their ears. I love how soft cats are and the contented way they purr.

"Here," Elena said, throwing a clean T-shirt to me. I changed and put the stained shirt in the hamper. Then we grabbed some sodas from the fridge and plopped onto the couch in the living room.

My dad also decorated the house, so the prints on the walls are panoramic cityscapes of Chicago, New York, and Houston, all with stormy skies and lightning bolts striking tall buildings. He framed newspaper articles, too — about different natural disasters like the tsunami in Indonesia and Hurricane Katrina in New Orleans. His prized possession is an article from 1900 when a hurricane hit Galveston and completely destroyed the town. He bought it on eBay. I don't know how much he paid, but it must have been a lot, because right after that, Mom threatened to cancel his eBay account.

"Do you think Nina wants to be our friend?" Elena asked.

"Not really," I said. "She doesn't like Courtney or Alicia, but I can tell she thinks Liz is cool. I'm sure she'd rather hang out with the in-crowd."

"If that's true, then why did she help us?"

"Because she's a decent person. But that doesn't mean she wants to be our friend. She probably felt sorry for us. Besides, she'd have a lot more fun with the in-crowd girls. I'm sure they do cool things like giving each other super-model makeovers or crank-calling the principal's house."

"How's that more fun than looking at ice-skating videos or playing Monopoly and Jenga?"

"Are you serious?" I said. "Where's my notebook?" I pulled it out of my backpack and turned to the next blank page. "The Top Five Reasons Elena Is a Nerd."

"Spare me, Windy."

"Five, her collection of Disney movie sound tracks."

"You mean the ones you borrowed last month?"

"Four," I went on, "her bunny rabbit slippers. Three, the encyclopedia of ice-skating stats she's got stored in her brain."

"At least I have a good memory."

"Two, Jenga and Monopoly on a Friday night."

"I don't play by myself, remember?"

"And the number one reason she's a nerd . . ."

Just then we heard a key in the front door.

"Hi, girls," my mom said as she came in.

We scooted over to make room for her on the couch. Like I said before, my mom is pretty. She has naturally arched brows and curled lashes that accentuate her dark eyes. Her face has no scars, zits, or freckles. She has the straightest, whitest teeth, which means she smiles a lot, which makes her even more beautiful. Usually, she wears her hair in a French twist, a braid, or a bun, but when she wears it down, it never frizzes like mine.

As soon as she sat down, she took off her shoes and socks. "My feet are killing me," she complained. "Do me a favor, Windy. Set up the VibraSpa, okay?"

"Okay," I said.

The VibraSpa is a little tub Mom bought at Walgreens. I put it beside her feet, poured in a pitcher of hot tap water, and turned it on. It made a light buzzing noise as Mom rolled up her pants to soak her feet.

"Oh, good. Nice and hot," she said when her first toe hit the water. She rubbed her soles against the little bumps on the bottom of the tub. "I feel a whole lot better."

"Nursing's too hard," I said. "You should have accepted that promotion last year. That way, you could work in an office instead of on your feet."

"So I could push papers around all day? I'd be bored."

"Better bored than tired."

She glanced at me. I could tell she wanted to scold me, but instead she grabbed a strand of my hair.

"What's this?" she asked when some red gunk got on her hands.

"I don't believe this," I cried. "I still have tomato sauce in my hair!"

"Do I still have some, too?" Elena ran to the bathroom mirror and I followed.

"Girls," Mom called. "What's going on?"

We returned to the living room. "We had a little accident," we said, and then we told her everything — how we tripped on the ice, how the kids laughed at us, how the new girl Nina helped out.

"It's all Elena's fault," I said.

"No, it isn't," she snapped back.

"You mentioned ice-skating. Where do you think they got that idea to trip us?"

"From their evil little minds," Elena said. "Besides, I'm proud of my dreams. I can't wait to do my presentation." She turned to my mom. "We're supposed to talk about our dream career."

"And which career did *you* pick?" Mom asked me.

I shrugged. "I don't really have any interests," I said.

"Yes, you do," Elena teased. "You've got a really, really *special* interest." She giggled. "His name's Ronnie."

"Elena!" I punched her arm. "I can't believe you said that."

"Ronnie?" Mom raised an eyebrow. "We'll have to discuss him later. But what about your speech? What do you want to be when you grow up?"

"Do I have to decide right now? I'm only in the eighth grade."

"When I was your age," Mom said, "I wanted to be an astronaut. I wanted to take a rocket ride into the sky."

Elena and I cracked up immediately. "Sorry, Mom," I said. "I can't imagine you traveling hundreds of miles per hour when you always drive *way* below the speed limit."

"And I can't imagine you floating in space with your hair all sticking up," Elena said.

"Floating in space sounds heavenly right now. At least my feet wouldn't hurt." Mom nodded toward the bathroom, her way of telling me to bring a towel. When I came back, she added, "Maybe I *am* afraid of going fast, but I seriously wanted to be an astronaut. The point is," she said as she lifted her feet from the tub to dry them, "I had an interest, a dream, something to work for and fantasize about."

"Like my ice-skating," Elena said.

Mom nodded. Then she looked at me. "There are a lot of careers related to the health field. Some people are nurses, but others are respiratory therapists, nutritionists, lab techs, or pathologists."

I squirmed at the thought of working with real live sick people. "Mrs. Campos said I should research office jobs," I said.

"That's a start. You might consider being a health insurance code specialist or a medical transcriptionist."

"A medscriptionist!" Elena announced, excited by her new word.

"I'll stop by the human resources department next week," Mom said. "I'll get some brochures for you."

"Wouldn't that be great?" Elena said. "You can work in the health field with your mom."

I rolled my eyes and grabbed my notebook, flipping to a list I had written weeks ago. "Five Good Reasons for *Not* Working in a Hospital."

Mom crossed her arms, as if daring me to continue.

"Five, bland hospital food. Four, cranky patients. Three, the alcohol smell. Two, killer germs. And one, tired feet."

"Ha, ha," Mom said, throwing the towel at me. "Just for that, I'm going to insist you volunteer this summer."

"Volunteer? You want me to work for free?"

"It's a good way to figure out your interests."

Elena jumped in, "That's a great idea! Maybe I can volunteer, too."

Honestly, sometimes I couldn't understand why she was my best friend. Best friends aren't supposed to sentence each other to a whole summer of work.

Just then, my father stepped in. He had a bunch of department store bags. "Hello, hello," he said as he placed the bags on the coffee table. "Just a sec." He went back outside and returned with even more bags.

"Alfonso," Mom said, a bit worried. "What have you been up to?"

"I left work early and went shopping."

Mom and I glanced at each other. Dad *never* went shopping.

"Let me show you what I got," he said, all excited.

He took out a shoe box and showed us a pair of black patent leather dress shoes. Then he unwrapped three suits. Three! Black, navy blue, and dark gray. He reached into a J. C. Penney bag and took out five white dress shirts and five pairs of black socks. Finally, he showcased a bunch of new ties — yellow with a blue paisley print, gray with navy swirls, a flowery tie, a striped tie, and a solid maroon one. Elena *ooh*ed and *aah*ed, but Mom and I were speechless.

"So what do you think?" Dad finally asked.

Mom scratched her head. "Well," she tried, but couldn't finish the sentence.

"I'm tired of wearing polo shirts and khakis all the time," he explained. "I need to look more professional."

Mom shrugged. She was as confused as I was.

"Watch the six o'clock news," Dad said, "with the new weatherman."

"The cute one with blond hair?" Elena asked.

"Yes. Him. He's good-looking, right? And he wears a suit every day."

"He *has* to wear a suit," Mom said. "He's on TV. But you're on the radio. No one sees you, so it doesn't matter what you wear."

Dad frowned. For the past ten years, he's been reporting the weather for a radio station — not the cool, pop station my friends listen to, but an AM station that makes local announcements like "mystery book club meets Tuesday at Westfall Library" or "please take your school supply donations to the yellow bus at Crossroads Mall." But now he says he wants to point at the high and low pressure systems, explain the satellite pictures, and announce his forecasts on TV every night. So when a television job came up, he applied. He got through his initial interviews, all the way to an audition tape. Only two applicants got that far, so my dad's chances were fifty-fifty. Unfortunately, he didn't get the job, which really confused us because sometimes the guy who *did* get the job stumbled over his words — something my dad would never, *ever* do.

"You bought this stuff in case another job comes up, right?" I asked.

"Yes," Dad admitted. "Remember last week, when the new guy predicted rain the same day I said that rain was unlikely? And *my* forecast was the right one?"

We nodded.

"You see? I do a better job of forecasting the weather. So why didn't I get the job? Then I realized — I didn't get the job because I don't look the part. So next time there's a position, I'll be ready."

"That's ridiculous," Mom said.

"It's the only explanation," Dad countered.

He was right. He *had* to be. All the popular girls wore headbands and plucked their eyebrows and used lipstick. They were "looking the part" just like the new weatherman.

"I don't believe it," Mom said.

"But it makes total sense," I added. "Right, Elena?"

Elena's face went blank. That girl could be so smart about numbers and science, but so dense about life.

"Why do you think we came home with tomato sauce all over our clothes?" I asked. "If we looked better, no one would pick on us."

"I don't know about you," she said, "but I look just fine."

"What's this about tomato sauce?" Dad wanted to know.

"Long story," I said, not wanting to explain again. "But since you're changing your style, can I change mine, too?"

"Sure," he said.

"So I can bleach my hair?"

"We've already discussed this," Mom replied, "and the answer is still no."

Dad nodded in agreement with Mom. "Besides, you have such lovely hair, *mija*."

"No, I don't. My hair looks like it's been in a tornado. I can never get rid of the tangles and frizz no matter what kind of conditioner I use. I just know you named me Windy because of my wild hair."

"No, I didn't," he said. "You were a *pelón*. Wasn't she, Isabel?"

Mom nodded. "You were so bald. We had to Scotch tape bows on your head so people would know you were a girl."

"Then why did you name me Windy?" I asked.

"Because we had gusts up to twenty-five miles per hour that day," Dad said.

"You named me after the forecast?"

Elena laughed. "Just be glad it wasn't humid or partly cloudy."

I guess I had to agree with her. It would have been a double bummer to be called "humid" all the time. At least Windy sounds a lot like Wendy, a *real* name.

"So what would you name a cat that had beige fur and the biggest, bluest eyes in the world?" I asked.

"Raindrop," Dad said.

Mom squinted at me, which meant she was suspicious. "Why are you asking about a cat?" She turned to Elena. "Why is my daughter asking about a cat?"

Elena gulped. She hated to lie, but she hated to get me in trouble, too.

"No reason," I said. "It's just a hypothetical question."

"I hope so." I could tell Mom wasn't satisfied. "You *better* be asking about a hypothetical cat. Because the last thing we need is another veterinarian bill."

"I know, Mom. You've told me a dozen times. No . . . more . . . cats." Keeping Raindrop was going to be a lot tougher than I realized.

I didn't think our conversation was over, but then Dad picked up his shopping bags, Mom collected the receipts, and Elena grabbed her phone to text her parents.

"Wait a minute! We're not finished yet."

Everyone stopped and looked at me.

"So can I bleach my hair?" I tried again.

Mom glanced at Dad. "Look what you started."

He sighed. "Your mother's right, *mija*. You can't bleach your hair, but if you want to buy some new clothes, that's okay. Just give me some time to save up. I went a little over my budget today." He gave an embarrassed chuckle before heading to his room.

I felt glad about the chance to go shopping, but I also knew that I would need a lot more than a new outfit to make me part of the in-crowd.

CHAPTER 4

Sleeper Hold

My dad often says he can smell a storm about to break even on the clearest day. "It's not a smell exactly," he once explained. "But a tension. Like the clouds sucking in the air, trying to hold it in, but getting all blue in the face before letting go of their breath."

I thought he was crazy till I felt that tension at school. Lots of people were holding their breath, getting ready to explode. The guys, for example. A lot of them liked Nina. She was new and pretty. She had no rep. She wore girly scarves but really rocked when it came to playing drums. The guys huddled at her locker, wanting to talk or carry her school supplies. She'd say, "That's so sweet," but she'd never stick around for a conversation or hand over her books. "I don't want them to get ideas," she once said. "Besides, I like high school boys. These kids are too young." That made sense because she'd be in high school if she hadn't been held back a year. "Not because I couldn't handle the work," she'd told me, "but because of my absences. I get headaches sometimes. A lot of times."

The in-crowd girls were holding their breath, too, since, with Nina around, the guys ignored them, even Courtney and Alicia, who'd been so popular. After Nina had challenged Courtney two weeks ago, the other in-crowd girls tried to be her friend, especially Liz. Maybe Courtney and Alicia had been mean to some of the in-crowd girls, too. Or maybe the in-crowd girls didn't want to be on Nina's bad side because she was quickly becoming the most popular girl in school. For some reason, though, Nina was more interested in hanging out with Elena and me — which made *us* hold our breath, because we knew she'd soon realize that being with us was a major social blunder.

In the meantime, we loved her attention. She constantly asked Elena about ice-skaters, and when she learned about Raindrop, she gave me a little blue collar for him. Plus, no one picked on us anymore. We were suddenly off-limits for the bullies and on-radar for Ronnie, who hovered nearby during lunch. Having him near made me feel prettier, even though my hair still frizzed and my glasses still fogged up every time I went outside. Because of Nina, I looked forward to going to school now, which made me feel smarter even though I hadn't cleared an A. But most importantly, I felt cool. A *real* kind of cool, not the fake high-maintenance cool of the in-crowd, but *coolicious*.

Unfortunately, having an in-crowd-worthy friend like Nina couldn't save me from speech class. Don't get me wrong, I liked the class — everything except for the speech-making part. On the first day of school, Mrs. Campos had said that the number two thing people feared was death and the number one thing was public speaking. I believed her. I changed my list for The Top Five Butterfly-in-the-Stomach Experiences and put public speaking at number one, right next to dressing out for P.E. I just hated the whole experience, so when Mrs. Campos asked for volunteers, I raised my hand first.

"Are you crazy?" Elena whispered.

"Going first and getting it over with is my motto," I explained.

"Mine's waiting and hoping we run out of time."

I was about to say her plan only made the misery last longer, but Mrs. Campos called on me.

"Okay, Windy," she said. "You can go first."

Our speeches required props. So I took my backpack to the front of the class and pulled out file folders, Post-its, a stapler, a calendar, pencils, pens, a sheet of white paper with a sketch of a keyboard (since my dad wouldn't let me bring his laptop), a tape recorder, Kleenex, and a telephone.

Just then, Courtney and Alicia walked in. Courtney carried a large cosmetic bag and a small boom box while Alicia was wrapped in a beach towel bigger than a twin-size sheet.

"You girls are late," Mrs. Campos said.

"We were getting ready," they explained, heading to their desks.

As Alicia passed Nina, I secretly hoped Nina would step on the ridiculous towel and trip her, but she didn't.

"Why don't you go ahead and start your presentation now," Mrs. Campos told me.

"Okay. I just have a few more things." I took out a coffee mug and framed pictures of El Niño, Cloudy, and Sunny. I placed them on the table with the other items, but since it looked messy, I tried to straighten up. The whole arrangement felt wrong, so I reorganized. That's when I realized that setting up a desk was truly complicated. Should the keyboard or the phone be easiest to reach? And should the file folders go on the left or right side? Where was the best place for the calendar? My hands shook and my foot frantically tapped the floor. I couldn't steady myself, so my props kept falling over. I straightened a file folder, but then my shaky hand knocked over the picture frame.

Suddenly Mrs. Campos cleared her throat to get my attention. When I looked up, Courtney rolled her eyes, and the rest of the students looked like they wanted to laugh. I got *so* nervous. The food in my stomach somersaulted like clothes in a dryer. I couldn't stop tapping my foot, and my sweaty palms could have ended a drought.

"Are you ready now?" Mrs. Campos asked.

"I just want to create a real desk environment, you know? I mean, um, not 'you know' but, well, um . . ."

Too many filler words! My score was sinking fast.

"Anyway," I began, "I researched the duties of a receptionist."

I held up the paper with my speech. I had a lot to talk about: the telephone, dictation, alphabetical order, scheduling. At home, my speech was exactly the minimum six minutes, but I must have talked really fast because my presentation was two minutes too short, which probably meant an additional ten points knocked off my score. Plus, I forgot to look at my audience. Oh, no! How many points would Mrs. Campos deduct for that? Hopefully I made a C. The school year was almost over, and I didn't want to repeat speech in summer school.

"That's it," I said. "That's all I have for my presentation."

I looked at all the bored people in the classroom. And then, I saw Nina. She smiled really big and clapped. Elena joined in, then Ronnie. Before I knew it, almost everyone was clapping, and even though Courtney and Alicia crossed their arms and glared, I didn't care. I'd never been applauded before. I knew my speech was crappy, but I felt like a celebrity.

After the applause, I restocked my backpack and returned to my desk. Courtney passed over a note with a sketch of a rabbit and "Way to go, Thumper" written underneath. I crumpled it. When I felt sure Mrs. Campos wasn't looking, I hurled the wadded paper, and it hit Courtney's "precious" face. *Score one for me*, I secretly cheered.

"I'll go next," Ronnie volunteered.

Mrs. Campos nodded, and the class waited as he organized some weight equipment. Then he started to unbutton his shirt.

"Ronnie," Mrs. Campos said nervously, "what are you doing?"

"Don't worry, Mrs. C," he said. "I wore a tank top underneath. Since I'm going to talk about the right way to train, I have to show my biceps."

"*Ooh!* Go ahead and show them," Courtney said. "We don't mind."

"Yeah! Why don't you show us how you train your abs, too?" Alicia added.

"Girls," Mrs. Campos warned.

"I'm sorry," Ronnie said. "I'm not trying to be improper or anything. I don't want to offend anybody. But since I'm going to be a trainer, I have to use my biceps as props."

"They can sure prop me up," Courtney said.

I pulled out my TOP FIVE notebook to fix my "Reasons I Hate Courtney and Alicia" list. I scratched out "Dressing Like Dallas Cowboy Cheerleaders on Western Spirit Day" and wrote "Flirting with Ronnie" instead.

"That's enough," Mrs. Campos told Courtney. Then turning to Ronnie, she said, "Are you ready to begin?"

He nodded as he picked up one of the bars. "This is a barbell. See how straight it is?" He put it back down and picked up a different bar. "This one is called an easy curl bar. See how it's, like, *not* straight?" Everyone nodded. "It's got this W in the middle, which changes the angle of your grip and makes it *easy* — get it? — to do *curls*, which is a really good exercise for your biceps."

First he showed us how to do preacher curls with the W-shaped bar. Then he showed us how to do standing barbell curls. And then he got the dumbbells and demon-strated concentration curls, hammer curls, and incline curls. This guy really knew how to work out his biceps. He kept pumping the weights, so his muscles got all firm and glisten-ing. I tried, but I couldn't stop my cheeks getting hot, my mouth getting dry, and my heart beating fast.

I didn't want the whole world to know how I felt about Ronnie, so I forced myself to look away. But Nina caught my eye. She must have seen me blushing because she held up a note. "Do you like him?" it read.

First I shook my head to say no, but then I nodded to say yes. When she smiled, I knew I could trust her, but since I wanted my feelings to stay secret, I made the sign for zipped lips. Nina answered with a thumbs-up.

A girl named Sonia went next. She spoke about *pan de polvo*, Mexican wedding cookies. They're usually covered with cinnamon sugar and shaped like hearts. Sonia's mom owns a bakery, and Sonia wants to expand the business by using different shapes like Christmas trees or pumpkins so people will order *pan de polvo* for other events, too. Lucky for us, she brought samples. They were delicious.

The next presentation was really dull. The boredom would have put me in a sleeper hold, but Nina clapped for it, too, which was a really nice thing to do.

Before the next person could volunteer, Nina raised her hand. "May I go to the restroom?" she asked.

Mrs. Campos nodded and handed her the hall pass.

When Nina opened the classroom door to leave, I saw Liz in the hallway and heard her say, "What took you so long?" Then Nina said, "Speeches." Then the door shut.

How strange. Why were they going to the restroom together? This question kept me from concentrating on the next two speeches but not from clapping. I really liked the applause because it made everyone feel good. We should have started the tradition months ago.

Nina finally returned. I wasn't timing her, not exactly, but she was gone for almost fifteen minutes. And maybe my eyes were playing tricks on me, but I felt positive her scarf had been knotted on the left side of her neck, not on the right as it was now. Maybe she took so long because she was trying different styles for her scarf. No matter how she wore it, she looked cool to me.

Finally, Alicia said, "I need to do my speech *today*, Mrs. Campos. This prom dress is on a strict eight-hour loan from my sister."

"Okay, you can go next," Mrs. Campos said.

Courtney took the boom box and a large cosmetic bag to the front of class while Alicia directed some students to push aside their desks to make a runway. Then she stood in front of class, staying wrapped in her towel. The only visible part of her outfit was the headband, light pink with some sparkly sequins.

"I'll demonstrate in a minute," she said. Whenever Alicia did a public speech, she punched out certain words. "First I want to give you some *facts* about *modeling*. It's not as easy as it looks. Models risk their *lives* to look good. They *starve* themselves to keep *skinny*." She nodded to Courtney who held up a poster about eating disorders. "*Anorexia* and *bulimia* are serious side effects of modeling. Did you know that in *Spain* there is now a minimum weight requirement for models?"

She glanced at Mrs. Campos who said, "That's very interesting, Alicia."

"I thought you'd like my public service announcement." Alicia focused on the class again. "Models bravely suffer the pain of plastic *surgery*, too. Just so they could look good for you." She snapped her fingers, and Courtney held up the next poster. "Here's some *vocabulary*. Rhinoplasty means *nose* job. Liposuction is the fancy word for *sucking* out *blubber*. And microdermabrasion means *sanding* away *pimples*. They sound painful, don't they? Well guess what . . . they *are*.

"But looking good is only half the job. Models work *sixteen* hours a day sometimes. They have to wear *bathing* suits even if it's cold outside. They have to walk in six-inch heels no matter how much their feet hurt. And they have to *smile* or look *sexy* through it all. It's tough, trust me." She looked at the class as if daring us to contradict her. "Now I'm going to demonstrate the proper way models walk."

She nodded at Courtney, who turned on the boom box. As soon as pop music started, Alicia threw off the towel to reveal her sister's prom dress. It was the lightest shade of pink with spaghetti straps, a slip style bodice, and a big bow on the behind. Her sister must have had a lot of curves because there was extra fabric around the chest and hips. The heels must have been her sister's, too, since Alicia walked like an amateur on a tightrope. She didn't care, though. She put her hands on her hips and smiled as if a dozen photographers were in the room. When one of the guys whistled, Alicia winked and threw him a kiss.

"That's enough," Mrs. Campos said. "You can stop your demonstration now. Here's your towel." I could tell she wanted Alicia to cover up again, but Alicia threw the towel aside.

Then she bowed. "That concludes my speech," she said.

Everyone lifted their hands to clap, but not Nina. Instead, she was examining her nails, pushing back her cuticles, all with a totally bored expression on her face. The class must have clapped three or four times before noticing Nina and then going completely silent. A full half minute passed. Mrs. Campos tried to stir up the applause. Courtney joined her, but everyone else followed Nina and stayed silent. First, Alicia's jaw dropped like someone surprised, then she looked down like someone with seriously hurt feelings.

"Okay, now," Mrs. Campos said. "Courtney? Why don't you go next?"

Courtney took a minute. She probably didn't want to do her speech, not after everyone had dissed her best friend. But she finally went to the front of class and prepped for her presentation. She patted Alicia's shoulder, and like a robot that had just turned on, Alicia removed her fancy headband and sat on a stool, while Courtney grabbed a big brush, a blow-dryer, a straightening iron, and a water bottle.

"In a real beauty salon," she began as she draped the beach towel over Alicia's shoulders, "the stylist washes the client's hair, but since we don't have a sink in here, I'll be wetting Alicia's hair with this water bottle."

Her voice trembled. Was she nervous? That would be a first.

She kept talking while she dampened Alicia's hair and clipped the upper layers so they wouldn't be in the way. And then, she turned on the hair-dryer. It was as loud as a helicopter! We saw her mouth move, but we couldn't hear a thing.

"Courtney," Mrs. Campos said. "Courtney!"

Courtney talked on. She didn't give eye contact since she was focused on the hair. Alicia squirmed in her seat, but she didn't interrupt her friend.

"*Courtney!*" Mrs. Campos shouted as she pulled the plug from the socket.

Courtney froze. "What's wrong?"

Mrs. Campos spoke gently now. "We couldn't hear you, hon. Would you like to try again?"

Courtney nodded, then restarted her speech. This time, she gave the class eye contact, first glancing at Nina, who was doodling on her book cover instead of paying attention. Maybe it was rude to act so bored, but why should Nina act interested? Why should any of us? Being a celebrity hairstylist was such a dumb idea.

"I . . . I . . ." Courtney was stumped. I should have felt sorry for her, but I didn't. I loved her confusion. For once, *she* looked like the fool. Eventually, she recovered and rushed through the rest of her speech. "That's it," she said after she made her last point.

"That's it?" Alicia whined. "Aren't you going to finish my hair?"

The class suddenly laughed because Alicia looked so funny. Half of her head was full-bodied and dry; the other half, flat and damp. Plus, she still had clumps of hair messily arranged in those non-glamorous hair clips stylists use.

Just then, the bell rang.

"We'll hear the rest of your speeches tomorrow," Mrs. Campos announced. "Class dismissed."

The students quickly left, but Elena and I took our time so we could eavesdrop on Courtney and Alicia.

"I look horrible," Alicia cried.

"At least your speech made sense," Courtney said.

"But I can't go to the cafeteria looking like this."

"Now, now girls," Mrs. Campos told them. "I don't have a class right now, so you can stay and get fixed up before going to lunch."

Elena and I giggled. "I can't believe they're crying about a bad hairdo," I whispered, "when we had to walk around with tomato sauce on our shirts."

Elena nodded as she handed me her gym bag. Once again, she had too much stuff. We finally moved toward the door, where Nina was waiting for us. We were about to leave when Courtney and Alicia called out.

"You did this," Alicia accused, pointing at Nina. "You ruined our speeches."

Nina shrugged. "I don't know what you're talking about."

"Yes, you do," Courtney said. "You told the class not to clap."

"I didn't tell them anything," Nina said, and it was the truth. What did Courtney and Alicia think? That we needed Nina's permission?

"You *had* to," Alicia said. "You passed a note or something."

Nina shrugged again. Then she held up the in-crowd's famous *W* sign and said, "Whatever."

CHAPTER 5

Pass-Out Game

On our way to the cafeteria, Elena said, "I feel sorry for Courtney and Alicia. I should have clapped."

"I can't believe you feel sorry for them," I said. "When do they ever care about *your* feelings?"

"Besides," Nina added, "it's not your fault Courtney brought a super-loud hair-dryer to class and then forgot to finish Alicia's hair."

I laughed again, remembering it. "Her hair looked like seaweed, didn't it?"

"Yeah," Nina said. "Serves her right, though."

"I can't believe you're being so meanormous," Elena said. "Alicia got really embarrassed. Courtney, too."

"Weren't *you* embarrassed?" Nina asked. "When you slipped on that ice?"

"Yeah, but . . ."

"That's how karma works. If you put out bad energy, that bad energy will come back and kick your butt."

"I guess," Elena said, though she didn't sound convinced.

"You're just too nice," I teased.

And Elena *was* too nice. That part was true. Most of the time, being nice was a good thing, but being *too* nice was the same as being foolish, right? After all, if karma didn't forgive and forget, then why should we?

We went through the cafeteria line, grabbed our trays, and found a table. As we ate, Nina gave us an overview of her upcoming speech. She planned to discuss drumming.

"What made you pick the drums?" Elena wanted to know.

"I knew all that banging would get on my mom's nerves," Nina joked. "Plus, pounding on the drums helps me let go of my frustrations."

"What are you frustrated about?" I asked.

"Lots of things. My parents are really busy, and it's like I'm invisible sometimes — except when they want to discipline me or something. And I really miss my breath sisters. I can't even talk to them on the phone anymore."

Elena and I glanced at each other. We still didn't know what *breath sisters* meant.

Just then, a group of in-crowd girls came by. They nodded and smiled at us. Usually, Elena and I are outright ignored, but without Alicia and Courtney around, some of the girls were actually nice, so I decided to smile and nod back. And the most wonderful thing happened! The girls acknowledged me, and Liz even said, "Stay cool."

"That was weird," Elena said. "Liz *never* pays attention to us." But it wasn't weird at all. If we were friends with Nina, and Nina was friends with Liz, didn't that mean Liz was friends with us? I couldn't be one hundred percent sure, but it was starting to feel that way.

After school, I stuffed my backpack with homework, and then made a pit stop at Elena's locker. Nina showed up, too. Once Elena had grabbed all her bags, we headed toward the exit.

"Do you walk home or take the bus?" Elena asked Nina.

"I take the bus."

"Really?" Elena said. "What's your bus number? I've never seen you in any of the lines."

"I ride the city bus," Nina explained. "I don't live in this district."

"You don't?" I said. "Then why do you come to school here?"

"Long story. Let's just say the teachers and parents wanted to take me away from my breath sisters."

This was the second time she mentioned breath sisters today. I was desperate to know what it meant.

"Is that some kind of sorority?" I asked. "I've heard of sororities in college, but not in middle school."

"I guess you could call it a sorority," Nina said. "Have you heard of blood brothers?"

Elena and I nodded.

"Breath sisters are just like blood brothers."

I still didn't get it. I knew blood brothers cut their palms and shook hands, but I couldn't imagine how to become a breath sister.

"My bus gets here in five minutes," Elena said.

On the days Elena didn't come to my house after school, I walked her to the bus line and then went home by myself, but the city stop was on the opposite corner of campus.

"I think I'll wait with Nina today," I decided. Before Elena could protest, I added, "So she can finish telling me about her speech."

"I still need to give my speech, too," Elena said.

"I know. I'll call later and we can talk about it then."

Elena glanced at me, then Nina, and then me again. I guess she thought I'd change my mind.

"I promise to call," I assured her.

"Well, okay," she said.

She left, but as she walked away, she turned around three or four times. For some reason, she made me think of my first day at school. Mom had taken me to the cafeteria for an assembly. After the principal introduced the teachers and welcomed the new students, I had to leave with my class. I kept looking back to make sure Mom was still there. I knew she'd pick me up in the afternoon, but part of me had worried she wouldn't.

Since the city bus stop was technically off campus, a few teachers would meet there to smoke. Elena and I called them Phlegm Masters. They'd go in the worst weather and spend their lunch breaks there, too. They smelled bad and had yellow teeth, but most of them were nice — except when they hogged up the shade and left the real bus riders in the sun. Nina and I nodded at them but stood a few feet away. Only out-crowd kids hung out with teachers.

"I can't wait till I start driving," Nina said. "Waiting for the bus is such a drag."

"Why don't your parents pick you up?"

"Are you kidding?" she said. "My dad is always out of town on business trips, and my mom has a five o'clock Pilates class. She'd rather skip ten years of her life than one hour of Pilates."

Some band kids walked by and said a few words to Nina. She was nice to all of them, even the double nerdy ones.

When Nina and I were alone again, I said, "So why did you and Liz sneak off today?"

"What do you mean?"

"During speech class. I saw her waiting in the hall."

"Oh, that." Nina fiddled with the edge of her scarf. "She wasn't waiting for me. We just happened to run into each other. A coincidence."

I was sure I heard Liz complain about Nina being late, but maybe I was wrong.

"You were gone for quite a while," I said.

"Was I?"

I nodded.

"You know how it is," Nina said. "Liz and I started talking and lost track of time."

I could completely relate. How many times had Elena and I lost track of time?

"Don't worry," I said. "Mrs. Campos was too busy with the speeches to notice."

Just then, Ronnie walked out of the school. He waved at us. Nina waved back and nudged me to do the same, but when I thought of his speech and his pumped biceps, my fingers and toes went numb.

"I thought you liked him," Nina said.

"I do, but . . . but . . ."

"So talk to him. It's not that hard. If you get stuck, ask a few questions. Trust me. Guys love to talk about themselves. And all you have to do is listen, or pretend to listen. He'll think you're the nicest person in the world. Even if you haven't said a word."

"Really?" I said. This seemed truly amazing — and simple.

"Hey, Ronnie," Nina called, waving him over.

He hurried to the bus stop.

"Hi, Nina," he said. "Hi, Trouper."

"Um, hi," I mumbled.

"So how'd you learn so much about training your biceps?" Nina asked.

"My uncle taught me. He's this massive bodybuilder. He's an eating, weightlifting machine. He works in a ware-house, so he can get *paid* to lift. All the skinny dudes use dollies or forklifts to pick up stuff. But not my uncle. He uses his *bare arms*. I'm not lying. His arms are as thick as most people's legs."

"Sounds like he's really strong," Nina said.

"Not really strong, but really, *really* strong. If my uncle was born a dog, he'd have the jaws of a pit bull and the muscles of a . . . of a . . . of another dog that was really, really strong. He even qualified for the regional bodybuilding contest in Austin next month."

He stopped. I waited for Nina to jump-start the conversation, but this time, she didn't say a word. When a few awkward moments passed, she poked my back. I got the hint and finally said something.

"I've never been to a bodybuilding contest. What's it like?"

"It's so cool! The dudes have to come up with a routine. They get to pick their own music and do their own choreography."

"Like ice-skaters?"

"No. I mean, they're not on ice or anything. They do this on a stage. And they don't wear those girly costumes. They wear Speedos."

"But they have judges, right?"

"Oh, yeah. Of course. They get scored. But that's only

part of it. After everyone does his routine, there's a pose-off where all the guys line up and do compulsory poses."

"What's a compulsory pose?" My questions were really flowing. Nina was right. I had Ronnie's full attention.

"There's a whole bunch of them. Like front double biceps." Ronnie lifted his arms and did the classic Popeye pose. "And the side chest pose." He turned slightly away, clasped his wrists in front of him, and squeezed his chest. "And the side triceps pose." He straightened his arm and flexed the muscles above the elbow.

Just then a truck drove up.

"Gotta go," Ronnie said. "That's my uncle. He's here to pick up the equipment I borrowed."

Thank goodness, I thought. I was getting all flushed and hot. One more compulsory pose and I'd pass out.

"See ya," Nina said to Ronnie.

"Sure thing," he answered. Then to me, he said, "Catch you tomorrow, Trouper." He punched me on the shoulder like I was his best gym pal. Then he bolted to his uncle, whose Ford pickup had tires as high as my shoulders.

"Those are the biggest muscles I've ever seen," Nina said as the uncle got out of the truck.

"If boulders could walk," I added, "they'd look something like him."

The Phlegm Masters finished their smokes and went back to the school, so Nina and I took over the bench.

"You're a real natural," Nina said. "See how Ronnie smiled once you got him talking? I can tell he likes you."

"Do you really think so? I've never seen 'Trouper' on a valentine."

"Trouper today. Sweetheart tomorrow. The best couples start off as friends."

That was a good point. Lovebirds *should* be friends first. I was starting to realize that Nina was a genius about people.

"There's my bus." She pointed down the street.

"Hey, Nina," I said, as she grabbed her backpack, "want to stay at my house Friday night? Elena will be there, too."

"Sorry, I can't. I'm permanently banned from sleepovers."

"Why?"

"My parents don't get the whole breath sister thing. And they're mad I was kicked out of my last school." The bus pulled up, the doors opened, and a few people stepped out. "But I can still hang out on Saturday. Let's make plans, okay?"

"Okay," I said.

She jumped on the bus, and the doors closed behind her. The last students had cleared the grounds. One custodian lowered the flag while another collected trash. I was all alone, so I had a quiet walk home.

When I finally got to my room, I pulled out my TOP FIVE notebook.

"What to Look for in a Friend," I wrote. "Five, someone cool, even with the in-crowd. Four, someone who listens. Three, someone who claps for you even after you give a crappy speech. Two, someone who has useful advice about boys."

I still didn't know what it meant, but for the number one thing to look for in a friend, I wrote, "Someone who'll be your breath sister."

CHAPTER 6

Wall Hit

The following Friday, Elena came by for a sleepover. We gathered all my cats, including Raindrop, and prepped them for a fashion show. "How hard could it be?" Elena said. But my cats refused to cooperate. They ran into the closet and under the bed instead. I couldn't blame them. They looked silly with the polka-dotted tube socks we put on their tails and the ribbons we tied on their legs. We even managed to saddle a birthday party hat on Cloudy.

At first I had fun, but after dealing with the hissing and wriggling and clawing, dressing up cats was just as lame as dressing up dolls. That was the weird thing about Elena. In some ways, her personality was as kid-like as her body. For example, she still wanted to trick-or-treat on Halloween. She still loved coloring books. And she still rode her bike along the sidewalk, a bike with tassels on the handlebars. Part of me loved hanging out with Elena, but another part of me felt embarrassed. I would never tell her, but sometimes I just wanted her to act like a normal eighth grader.

After dressing up the cats, we spent the rest of the night redecorating my room because it seriously needed to grow up, too. "The Top Five Most Embarrassing Details About My Room," said page 29 of my TOP FIVE notebook. "Five, the ruffled, pink comforter. Four, the plastic Playskool oven. Three, the row of five-by-seven school portraits hanging above my bed. Two, a dozen teddy bears in my old bassinet, all with chewed-off ears. And the number one most embarrassing detail of my room: a tangle of permanent marker squiggles I drew on the wall when I was six."

Yup, my room seriously needed an update. The only thing I liked about it was a corkboard where I tacked mementos like ticket stubs from the Stars on Ice show; the *calavera*, or skull, card from my Mexican bingo set; and a filmstrip of pictures Elena and I had taken at the mall. We smiled in one picture, crossed our eyes in another, stuck out our tongues in a third, and tried, but failed, to look serious in the fourth. Next to them, I wrote "BFF."

"Let's get busy," I said.

Elena and I took down my goofy school pictures and covered the walls, including the embarrassing squiggle marks, with the heartthrob posters from my teen magazines. We got rid of the frilly bedspread and dressed up the plain purple sheets with decorative pillows. We carried the plastic stove to the garage, so I could make some money at our next garage sale.

"What about this bassinet?" Elena asked.

I looked at all the teddy bears snuggled within it. "I'm going to keep it after all. Too much sentimental value."

After working on my room, we talked late into the night — mostly about Ronnie, how cute he was.

"Who do *you* like?" I asked.

She listed a bunch of ice-skaters. "They're supercute in those tight outfits they wear. Plus, they have talent."

"But they aren't real people. You don't *know* them."

"Of course they're real. I've got autographs, remember? I know them by the way they interpret the music, by the way they dance."

I threw a pillow at her. "You are so corny!"

She just sighed as she told me about her favorite skaters and routines. She went on and on. All I heard was Elena's voice and Raindrop's purrs. At some point, nothing made sense anymore. My consciousness hit a wall and I conked out.

*   *   *

The next morning, I had a little trouble waking up.

"Girls!" Mom called. "We're leaving in five minutes."

She was taking us to Pleasant Hill, the assisted living place where she worked. Nina planned to meet us there so we could go to the mall afterward. Well, so Nina and I could go. Elena had to visit her grandma.

"Okay," I called back. Then to Elena, I said, "Hurry. Give me Raindrop before my mom peeks in."

Raindrop had made a home in the bushes outside my window. We had a little routine now. I fed him outside before and after school. Then, right before bed, I let him in, and he slept on my extra pillow. My window wasn't high off the ground, and since cats always landed on their feet, I could safely drop Raindrop outside.

"Remember," I told Elena, "you can't let my mom know about the cat."

"Of course," she said.

We began to pack her suitcase, backpack, and ice chest.

"Why did you bring so much stuff?" I complained. "This was a sleepover, not a vacation."

"I believe in being prepared."

"You call this being prepared?" I held up an empty CD

case. "And what's this for?" I pointed to a vial of candy sprinkles and a Ziploc of crushed pecans.

"I thought we might want to make cookies. And I brought this sewing kit just in case a button fell off. The flashlight is for a power outage, and the Nutty Buddy Bars, peanut butter cheese crackers, pickles, popcorn, and carrot sticks were for midnight snacks, in case we got hungry. I brought my backpack and all our textbooks because we might've wanted to study if we got bored."

"We *never* study when you spend the night," I said. "Even when we're supposed to."

"Trust me, Windy, the one time I don't bring my books, we'll be in the mood to study, and the one time I forget my exercise DVD, we'll feel like doing aerobics, and the one time I leave my *Los Barrios* cookbook at home, we'll feel like making pumpkin *empanadas*."

"But did you have to bring your Mini-Vac, too?"

"Of course. What if we made a mess?"

"Girls!" Mom called again. "I'm going to be late if you don't hurry up."

"In a minute, Mom."

Just then, she came to the bedroom door. "I've got to leave *right* now," she said, pointing at her watch. "You don't want to be late for your new friend, do you?"

69

"Okay, okay," we said.

While I grabbed Elena's suitcase and while Mom grabbed her ice chest, Elena slipped her arms through her backpack and purse, tucked her pillow beneath her arm, and with her free hands, picked up her piccolo and the case with her portable DVD player. We lugged Elena's stuff to the car, cramming everything but the piccolo into the trunk. Then we clicked on our seat belts and headed to Pleasant Hill, so I could spend time with Mrs. Vargas.

I'm lucky enough to have three grandmothers — my two *abuelas* from Mom and Dad, and my adopt-a-grandma, Mrs. Vargas. I've been visiting her since I was ten, the year Pleasant Hill sponsored an Adopt-a-Grandparent program. The old people had lined up along one side of the rec room while the kids lined up along the other. Then the kids reached into a sack to pull out their adopted grandparent's name. At first, I felt shy about hanging out with Mrs. Vargas, but after we went Christmas caroling with the other Adopt-a-Grandparent pairs, I realized that she was one of the sweetest people on the planet. And we've been friends ever since.

"So," Mom said to Elena when she reached the first stoplight, "do you have any plans for summer?"

"Yes, I'm going to band camp. I went last year and had a superific time."

"Superific?"

"Super *and* terrific. Get it?"

Mom nodded and laughed. "Maybe there's a camp for you, too, Windy."

"I don't think so, Mom."

"It doesn't hurt to investigate. Isn't there a space camp in Alabama?"

"*You're* the one with the astronaut dreams. Not me. All *I* want to do this summer is watch soap operas and buy cold *raspas* when the snow cone truck comes by."

"Soap operas and *raspas* are not interests," Mom said. "Don't you think you'd have fun at something like a band camp?"

"Maybe. If I played an instrument."

"I *love* playing my piccolo," Elena said. "Right now, we're practicing famous movie tunes for the spring concert. Like the themes for *Star Wars* and *The Simpsons*."

"Do you get to play any solos?" Mom asked.

"No. There isn't much for a piccolo to do, but Nina has a really cool solo. She gets to do Indian drumbeats from this movie called *Last of the Mohicans*. It's mag-tastic."

"Sounds like she's talented. I'm glad I'll get to meet her." Mom then focused on me again. "See, Windy? All your friends have interests. There has to be *something* you like to do."

I rolled my eyes. "You're taking this too seriously, Mom."

"I'm just saying you should try different things. Get a hobby like the rest of us. You didn't even look at the health career brochures I gave you."

"I looked at them. I already did my presentation, didn't I?"

Mom pulled into the employee parking lot. "I want you to ask your counselor about summer camps," she decided.

All I could do was roll my eyes again.

We got out of the car and walked toward the building. Pleasant Hill is a three-story retirement home with walls made of large, irregularly shaped stones. It's built like a square horseshoe with a courtyard in the middle. By the front door is a circular drive where a van picks up the residents for outings, and toward the back is another, more secluded drive for the ambulances. Sometimes, instead of an ambulance, I'll see a hearse.

Mrs. Vargas lives on the first floor. She has diabetes, so the nurses constantly monitor her insulin and diet. "And they clip my toenails, too," she once told me. Other than that, she can take care of herself. In fact, her room is like an apartment, with its own bathroom and kitchenette. Only the PA system reminds me that we're in a hospital. When Mrs. Vargas wants company, she goes to the general area and watches CNN. Sometimes she does crafts or plays card games and Scrabble with her friends.

"There's Nina," Elena said, and sure enough Nina was waiting by the front door. She wore black jeans, a white shirt, and a solid red scarf.

I introduced her to my mom.

"Hello, Mrs. Soto," Nina said as she shook my mom's hand. "It's a pleasure to meet you. Windy and Elena have been really nice to me at school. It's tough joining the class so late in the year."

"I'm sure it is," Mom said. "Where are your parents? I was hoping to meet them."

"They wanted to meet you, too," Nina replied, "but my dad's out of town and my mom had a lot of errands to run, so she just dropped me off."

"Well, we *are* a little late." Mom glanced at me and Elena as if to say, "I told you so." She walked us inside, and when we got to the elevators, she said, "You girls have fun. Windy's dad is going to pick you up in a couple of hours."

We waved as she disappeared behind the elevator doors. Then we went directly to Mrs. Vargas's room.

As soon as she saw Elena and me, she hugged and kissed us. "Who's this?" she asked about Nina.

"Our new friend."

"Hello, 'new friend.' Come in. Come in. What's your name?"

"Nina. I go to school with Windy and Elena."

"Well, any friend of Windy's is a friend of mine. Isn't that right, girls?"

We nodded.

"Come and help me with this puzzle." We followed her to a table next to a sliding door that opened onto the court-yard. "I'm having lots of trouble with the sky part."

Mrs. Vargas loves 1,000-piece puzzles. Most of them are landscapes of beautiful places — cottages surrounded by ice-capped mountains, seascapes with colorful sailboats, or villages with cobblestone roads. She decoupages over her favorite scenes, then frames them and hangs them on the wall.

"We had our speech presentations last week," Elena said. "Ronnie, the guy Windy likes, showed us how to lift weights, and I talked about ice-skating."

"And Windy?" Mrs. Vargas asked.

Nina answered for me. "She did a great job telling us about office jobs."

"That's right," I said. "I focused on receptionist duties." Mrs. Vargas had trouble hearing, so when she didn't respond, I said, "Did you hear me?"

"Yes," she answered. "So what did the receptionist say?"

"Nothing. I mean, I was telling you about my speech presentation."

"What speech presentation?"

She *never* got this confused. I felt embarrassed since Nina was here. I didn't want her to think Mrs. Vargas was senile.

"Are you feeling okay?" I asked.

Mrs. Vargas put down the puzzle piece and sighed deeply. "I just can't concentrate today."

"Why not?" Elena said. "Are you feeling sick? Do you need a nurse?"

"No. I'll be okay. It's just . . . seeing you three . . . makes me think of all the friends I've had over the years . . . of Mrs. Williams. Remember her?"

"She had the room across the hall, right?" I said.

"Yes, but she's been on the second floor for a long time. Now she's on the third floor because she had a stroke."

I've never been to the third floor, but the second floor is where Mom works. It has a strange mix of alcohol and vegetable broth smells. It also has the constant beeps of call buttons because the patients need help with walking, dressing, taking a bath, or eating. My poor mom walks back and forth all day, making sure her patients are clean, fed, and given the correct medicines. She takes their temperature and blood pressure and scribbles on their charts. She fills their water pitchers, fluffs their pillows, and delivers their magazines and lunch trays. She works harder than anyone I know, and the only thing she complains about is her feet. Only a person as special as Mom could handle nursing all these years. So I admired her. I really did. But I also thought it was time for her to try another kind of job — an office job.

"What's on the third floor?" Nina asked.

"Oh, honey," Mrs. Vargas cried. "We call it the last stop before heaven." She put her hands over her face and sobbed a little. Elena quickly handed her a tissue.

Now I knew why Mom never talked about the third floor. A lot of her patients must have died over the years. When her feet hurt, her heart must hurt, too.

"Don't cry," Elena said.

"I don't mean to ruin your visit," Mrs. Vargas apologized. "I just wish my friends could stay on the first floor forever. I like having them nearby when I need to talk."

"I understand," I said. "But I'm your friend, too. You can always call *me*. That's what *we* do, right?"

Elena and Nina nodded.

"When I feel bad," Nina said. "I bang on my drums."

"I pet my cats," I said.

"And I play my piccolo," Elena added.

"Your Pinocchio?" Mrs. Vargas said.

"No." Elena laughed. "My *piccolo*." She opened her case and took out the instrument. "We all have to close our eyes. It's the only way to feel the music."

We did as Elena asked, and she began to play. The notes jumped lightly up and down, and in my imagination, I saw an orange balloon. Not a helium balloon that floats away, but a regular birthday party balloon, slowly bouncing as a child played volleyball with it. Then Elena played a more energetic piece, and I imagined Raindrop chasing a ball of yarn.

When Elena finished, she asked Mrs. Vargas, "Where did you go?"

"I was the red umbrella. I was that beautiful splash of color in that puzzle over there." She pointed above her dresser to a picture of a busy, rainy street with one red umbrella in the black-and-white scene. Nina was standing near it.

"How did you get over there?" I asked. She'd been sitting at the table when Elena began the music.

"Just felt like dancing," she explained.

"See why I carry so much stuff?" Elena said. "You never know when you're going to need it. I made Mrs. Vargas smile and Nina dance. That's why you should always be . . ."

"Prepared," I said. "Do you know you're starting to sound like my mother?"

We got back to the puzzle, and little by little, Mrs. Vargas cheered up. I knew we couldn't stop her friend from being on the third floor, but at least we could make her forget her troubles for a while.

CHAPTER 7

Cloud Nine

We walked out of Pleasant Hill and discovered that Dad had switched cars with Mom so we wouldn't have to transfer Elena's stuff. When he saw us approaching, he got out of the car.

"Dad!" I exclaimed. "What did you do to your hair?" Normally, my dad has dark brown hair, a little long and unruly on top, but that day, his hair was superlight, almost orange.

"I went to HairQuest. Thought it was time for a change."

I couldn't believe this. Dad wouldn't let me lighten my hair, but the first chance he got, he lightened his.

"You know I've wanted to change my hair since forever," I complained.

He glanced at Nina. "We'll talk about this later," he said. I figured he probably didn't want to argue in front of someone new.

Just then, Nina held out her hand and introduced herself. "Thanks for giving us a ride to the mall," she said, all pleasant. "HairQuest is a great place. Sometimes I go there, too."

Dad nodded, then held open the door so Nina and Elena could climb into the backseat. Once they were in, he held open the front door for me. He was acting like such a gentleman, but I was still mad.

When he started the car, I heard the familiar radio jingle of the station where he works. Then a doctor started an infomercial about a dry skin remedy. Every five seconds, Dad glanced at himself in the rearview mirror.

Did he really think he looked better? How could he betray me this way? What about *my* new style? Why couldn't I change *my* hair? I couldn't believe how ridiculous Dad looked, wearing his fancy suit on a Saturday when he didn't even have to go to work.

Elena and Nina chatted and giggled about the other girls at school, but I was too angry to join in. Instead I took out my TOP FIVE notebook, secretly hoping Dad would notice. But he was too busy listening to the infomercial and glancing at his new hair.

"The Top Five Reasons for Throwing a Sheet over Dad," I wrote. "Five, his hair looks orange. Four, he looks like a traffic cone with ears. Three, rats might think he's cheese. Two, he's not looking at the road anyway, so why does he need to see? And the number one reason to throw a sheet over Dad? Can I have a drum roll, please? He's a hypocrite. A well-dressed hypocrite with Ronald McDonald hair!"

Okay, maybe his hair wasn't as bright as Ronald McDonald's, but when I got mad, I tended to exaggerate.

I finished my list just as we got to Elena's house. As soon as Dad turned off the car, she said, "I'm going to ask if I can go to the mall with you guys." Then she sprinted to her door.

"I thought her grandma was coming over," I said. I didn't intend to sound eager to leave her behind, but that's how it came out. Besides, I had spent the whole night and most of the day with her. Now it was time for me to spend time with Nina. How did that saying go? "Two's company but three's a crowd." That was how I felt when Elena was around because every time I tried to be cool, she always said something nerdy.

Dad opened the trunk, and we grabbed some of Elena's things. A minute later, she came back out. She wasn't sprinting anymore. She walked like someone giving a piggyback ride to a laundry bag full of wet towels.

"My mom said no," she told us as she brushed by.

Elena's mom held open the door so we could put the bags inside. Soon Elena returned with the rest of her stuff.

"I hate when Grandma comes," she mumbled. "It's not like she talks to me or anything."

"Young lady," her mom warned.

"Well, it's true. She can barely hear anything."

"She can hear well enough. You just have to look at her when you speak."

My dad, Nina, and I stood around. Nothing was more uncomfortable than watching someone else's family squabbling.

"Thanks for bringing her home," Mrs. Sheppard said.

"My pleasure," Dad answered.

"Bye, Elena," I called. "We'll catch you next time."

She gave me a halfhearted wave good-bye, and then turned away.

She seemed mad at me. She *was* mad at me. After all these years of friendship, I could tell. What was the big deal about missing one afternoon?

Dad left Nina and me at North Star Mall. Nina's mom was going to pick us up and take me home. I couldn't wait to meet her. She was probably double cool, unlike my silly-looking dad.

"I hope you don't think my dad's weird," I told Nina as he drove off.

"Why?" she asked. "Because he lightened his hair?"

I covered my face with my hands, all embarrassed.

"I thought your dad's hair looked great," Nina said.

"Really?"

"Yeah. At least he *has* hair. My dad is going bald."

"Thing is," I said, "my dad never cared about the way he looked. Now, all of a sudden, he's obsessed about it. It wouldn't bother me if he'd let me bleach *my* hair."

"Why would you want to bleach it? Your hair looks beautiful just the way it is."

"You really think so?"

"Would I lie to you?" She looked straight into my eyes.

"No," I answered. "I guess not."

"So it's settled then. You've got good hair."

Part of me didn't accept this. I always thought my hair was a frizzy, tangled mess. But as we approached the glass door to the mall, I saw my reflection. My hair was a deep brown and full-bodied. Maybe it did look beautiful — kind of.

We stepped into the mall and a cold blast of air hit our faces.

"Come on," Nina said. "Let's eat. I'm starved."

We went directly to the food court and ordered Chinese from Panda Express. Nina got rice with sweet and sour chicken, and I got rice with sweet and sour pork.

We found a table and started eating. Then I opened my TOP FIVE notebook so we could make lists — The Top Five Toppings for Ice Cream, The Top Five Coolest Colors for Tennis Shoes, The Top Five Grossest Things to Find Beneath Your Fingernails, The Top Five Uses for a Packet of Ketchup, and The Top Five Embarrassing Things People Do in a Food Court When They Think No One's Looking.

"I'm going to get a refill," I said. "Would you like one?"

"Sure." Nina handed me her cup.

When I returned, she quickly closed my notebook.

"Did you make another list?" I asked.

"No. But I found one that wasn't finished, so I added to it."

I riffled the pages to find it. I couldn't believe I'd left an incomplete list.

"You can read it later," she said. "I've got a cool idea."

"Really? What is it?"

"Let's get makeovers."

Our drama teacher had two masks at the top corners of her door. I could feel those masks on my face as I went from smiling to frowning. "My parents don't want me to wear makeup yet," I said. "I've got to be in high school first."

"It's just for today," she said. "You can wash it off before you go home."

She was right. I could always wash it off. If Dad could try a new hair color, then I could try a little makeup. It was only fair. Besides, getting a makeover sounded like a lot of fun. Elena *never* had good ideas like this.

We went to Dillard's. As we walked through the cosmetics department, a lady offered to squirt us with perfume, so we held out our wrists. The mist was cool, and I liked the floral scent even though it made me sneeze.

"This is really expensive," I said, glancing at the prices on the makeup containers.

"Don't worry. My treat."

"Oh, no. I couldn't, Nina."

"It's not a problem. I *owe* you, remember?"

"For what?"

"For being my friend. I was the new kid at school, and you made me feel right at home. I was really lucky to meet you."

Wow! Her compliment put me on cloud nine. If I kept

hanging out with Nina, I'd be in the in-crowd before the semester ended. I just knew it.

"I guess you can treat me, then," I said. "But let's look at the clearance or the discontinued stuff."

Nina agreed and bought me a brown eyeliner, a very natural-looking lip gloss, a compact that was the exact shade of my skin, and a bottle of clear polish for my nails. The total was over $20, but she paid. I figured her parents must have a lot of money.

"Let's go to the restroom," Nina said, heading to the hallway behind the customer service counter.

The restroom at Dillard's had a parlor with a small sofa, a coffee table, an arrangement of fresh flowers, and a huge gold-framed mirror. Another door led to a room with silver stall doors, and sinks that were nestled in a black marble countertop that almost looked like a mirror because it was so clean. The whole place smelled like lavender. And everything was no-touch. Just wave the hand beneath the faucet for water or under the dispenser for soap.

First, I washed my face. Then we sat on the sofa in the parlor. Nina took the compact and brushed the powder onto my face. It tickled the way Raindrop's fur tickled when he nuzzled against my neck. Next, she told me to close my eyes as she applied the eyeliner. I could feel her body warmth as she leaned close and smell the perfume that lingered on her wrists. Finally, she handed me the lip gloss, telling me to use just a little bit.

"You look great," she said.

I looked at my reflection in the mirror. I *did* look great. Nina was right, again. My skin looked smoother, my lips fuller, and my eyes more defined.

"You think Ronnie will notice?" I asked.

"Are you kidding? He's been noticing you all week."

It was true. Ever since our conversation at the bus stop, Ronnie had found me in the cafeteria or hallway and talked to me. A lot.

"Let's do your nails," Nina said.

She took a file from her purse and shaped my nails, rounding the edges and making them all even. Then she opened the bottle of clear polish. For a while, the chemical smell overpowered the lavender, but I got used to it. Nina took the little brush and swept it over my nails. Then she blew on them, her breath like autumn's first cool front, the one that reminds you that the sweets and gifts of Halloween and Christmas are only a few weeks away.

I knew it was a stupid question, but I had to ask. "Is this how you become a breath sister?"

She laughed a little, and I felt like a kid who still believes thunder is the sound of angels bowling.

"I thought you knew what a breath sister was," she said.

"I do. It's like being a blood brother, right?"

"The concept's the same."

I stared at her, waiting for more.

She stopped blowing on my nails but still held my hands. Then she asked, "Have you ever heard of the choking game?"

CHAPTER 8

The Choking Game

I know about metaphors. We talk about them in English class. Metaphors happen when people say something that really stands for something else. Like when you say "letting the cat out of the bag" or "spilling the beans" instead of "telling a secret." There isn't a cat in a bag, and there aren't any beans on the ground. It's all figurative. So I thought that "choking game" was a metaphor. But it wasn't.

"It's got other names," Nina said. "Like Knockout Game, Wall Hit, Airplaning, Rocket Ride."

"I've never heard of them."

"How about Sleeper Hold, Pass-Out Game, or Cloud Nine?"

I shook my head to all of these.

"I can't believe it," she said, laughing. "Where have you been all this time?"

"Hanging out with Elena," I said.

"Oh, right. Hanging out with Elena." The way she said it made it sound like hanging out with Elena equaled playing on the merry-go-round — which made sense, since it was true.

"So what's it like?" I asked. "This choking game?"

"You want to try it?"

"Will it make us breath sisters?"

"For life," she said.

"Okay, then. Let's do it."

"First you have to swear to secrecy," she said. "I already got kicked out of school for this, so you can't tell anyone — not even Elena."

I had to think a moment because Elena and I tell each other everything, even our dreams, no matter how strange. Like the time I dreamed Courtney and Alicia were pointing at me because I went to school as the Statue of Liberty, and like the statue, I was frozen, so I couldn't speak or throw away the torch and crown. Then Courtney painted embarrassing graffiti on me, and everyone laughed. When I told Elena, she didn't think I was weird or say that my dream was one big freak-o-rama. She listened. She said she had bad dreams about Courtney and Alicia, too.

I had never considered keeping a secret from her. But all of a sudden, I didn't *want* to tell her everything. I knew I'd keep the choking game private because I wanted to share something with Nina, with *only* her.

"I promise not to tell," I said.

Nina smiled, picked up our things, and led me to the restroom, checking beneath the stalls to make sure we were alone. Then we went to the largest stall, the one for ladies in wheelchairs. Nina secured the latch and looped our purse straps on the door hook.

"The choking game's about trust," she said. "So you have to trust me." She put her hands on my shoulders, and looked me straight in the eyes. "Do you trust me with your life?"

The daredevil feeling that came from walking through the park at night or racing my bike down a steep hill washed over me.

"Yes," I said. "Do you trust *me*?"

"One hundred percent," Nina replied.

"Then teach me how to play the choking game."

She took my hand and placed my fingers on the side of my neck.

"Feel that?" she asked.

I felt my skin's warmth and my pulse.

"It's like a water hose in your neck," she said. "When we play the choking game, we pinch off the flow."

I backed up a few steps. "You want to strangle me?"

"Windy." She laughed. "What did you think? It's called the *choking* game."

"But . . ."

"You're not going to get hurt," she said. "I've played it lots of times. Do I look hurt to you?"

I shook my head. "But people *die* from being choked."

"Only if you keep holding on," she said. "That's why we have to trust each other and let go before the game goes too far. That's what makes us breath sisters — we put our lives in each other's hands. Can you think of a better way to prove your friendship?"

Her explanation made sense. Then again, I never had to prove my friendship to Elena, so why did I have to prove it here?

"You can tap out whenever you want," Nina said.

"What does that mean?"

"If you want me to stop, you can tap my arm and I'll let go."

Just then, we heard someone come into the restroom, and Nina made the sign for keeping quiet. The interruption gave me time to think about what it meant to be a breath sister, to *become* one, which made me think about the way blood brothers would take a knife, slash their palms, and shake hands. That had to hurt, not to mention all the germs. At least you didn't bleed when you played the choking game. So how bad could it be? And if other girls were doing it, then it must be okay. Plus, it gave you a really special friend, an *in-crowd* friend.

As soon as the lady washed her hands and left, Nina said, "You don't have to play if you don't want to, but it's the only way we can be official breath sisters."

I felt scared, but even though I knew I might get hurt, a sense of adventure kept me going. "I know," I said. "I thought about it. And I'm ready."

She smiled. "Just remember, you can tap out whenever you want."

"Okay," I said.

Nina approached me, and I felt a little sick — like before a presentation in speech class. But I really wanted to do this, so I took a deep breath and nodded to give her the okay. She pressed her hands on both sides of my neck and started to squeeze. Just a little at first, but when I didn't stop her, she squeezed tighter. I smelled the perfume on her wrists again, but since it'd been there for a while, it seemed sour now. Then I felt her breath, a light breeze, and I liked it, liked being close to her even if it meant playing this weird game. Then she squeezed my neck even tighter. It didn't hurt but I felt pressure in my head like when I used to hang upside down on the monkey bars too long. Then the pressure started to balloon, especially behind my eyes. Was my head going to explode? Because that was how it felt. I started to panic. *Let go!* I tried to say. But I couldn't because my voice was choked off, too. Then a bunch of green dots appeared. I knew I'd faint if I didn't tap out. So I slapped at Nina's forearms, and immediately, she let go — just like she promised.

I gasped and waved her off.

"You did great," Nina said. "Maybe next time you'll go all the way."

I couldn't speak yet, so I gave her a questioning look because I wanted to know what "all the way" meant.

"You're supposed to pass out," she said. "That's how you get the rush."

"What rush?" I managed.

"That high, floaty feeling. That's why people play this game."

I rubbed my neck. I could still feel the heat and pressure from her hands.

"Stay here," she said. "I saw a vending machine outside. I'll go get you some water."

I could have waited in the parlor, but I was too afraid to leave the stall. People would see me, and they'd know what I'd been up to. I took out the compact Nina bought me and looked in the mirror. My neck was red, but already, the redness was going away. After a few more minutes, I could hide my act from the world and erase every trace of the choking game.

The only thing I could not erase was how I felt. As soon as I left the restroom stall, I'd be leaving a version of myself behind — because — because I was different now. I'd changed, like the way I'd changed after my first day in kindergarten or after Cyclone, my first cat, died. The way I imagined I'd change if I ever got to kiss Ronnie or drive a car. I felt smarter now, more grown-up.

Finally, Nina returned with a bottle of water. She even opened it for me. I nearly drank the whole thing.

"Are you okay?" she asked.

"Sure," I said, wishing I sounded more confident.

We left the restroom. Nina carried my purse and the bag of new makeup. I felt so confused. I really wanted to be Nina's friend. I didn't like the choking game, but everything else we did was fun.

"How many times do I have to play the choking game?" I asked.

"You don't have to play again if you don't want to," she said. "Do you want to?"

I shook my head. "Do *you* play a lot?"

"Not a lot. But sometimes."

I rubbed my neck. It felt a little sore.

"Hey, I've got another great idea," she said. "Since we're breath sisters now, let's buy matching scarves."

I brightened up. "You mean it?"

"Yeah. It'll be so cool. We can wear them on the same day."

I must have smiled really big because she grabbed my hand and pulled me to the accessories department. There were two aisles of beautiful scarves — some with fringe, some with sequins, some with detailed patterns, others with no pattern at all, just solid color. Choosing a design was tough, but since we didn't have a lot of money, we settled for scarves from the discount bin, finding two yellow ones that were a complete match.

After we paid for them, Nina said, "This day has been so much fun, Windy."

When I heard this, I didn't feel confused anymore. Nina was my friend now — more than that, my breath sister.

CHAPTER 9

American Dream Game

"We better hurry," Nina said, "or we'll miss our buses home."

Buses? That wasn't part of our plan. "I thought your mom was going to pick us up," I said.

Nina laughed as if I'd made a joke.

"What's so funny?" I asked.

"Don't you remember, Windy? I'm grounded. I'm not supposed to be at the mall today. I'm supposed to be volunteering at the old folks' home."

I remembered now. She *had* told me she was grounded. But she said she was grounded from sleepovers. She hadn't mentioned the mall.

"My parents think your mom's picking us up," I complained. "They think they'll meet her."

"They *will*. Next time." She must have seen me frown. "Sometimes you have to tell people what they want to hear," she added. "Would your parents let you hang out with someone who was in trouble?"

"No."

"Okay, then."

We continued through the mall, shouldering past slower people and occasionally bumping into mothers with strollers that seemed built for shopping bags instead of babies.

I didn't like to lie. It made me nervous. I *always* got caught. Plus, I felt so guilty, especially when I lied to my parents. As far as I could tell, they had always told me the truth, even about tough things. Like, after my cat Cyclone died, I asked if I'd die, too. They said yes. I was five or six at the time, so that kind of info really hurt. But they gave it to me anyway.

Nina found the exit, and soon we were near the bus stop.

"Thanks a lot," I mumbled.

"What's wrong?" she asked.

"My mom and dad will be waiting," I said. "They probably made coffee. Now *I'm* going to get grounded when your mom doesn't show up."

"No you won't," she said. "Just tell your parents we were in a hurry. We dropped you off at the corner so we wouldn't have to turn into your street. Tell them they'll meet my mom the next time and mention that she was really disappointed about not getting to visit."

"You don't get it, Nina. I'm not good at lying. My parents can *read* me. It's like I've got a marquee on my forehead. Every time I lie, my forehead tells the truth."

"Always?" she asked.

"Yes."

"What about Raindrop?"

I hated to admit it, but she was right. I *had* lied about Raindrop. But that was a different situation. I was protecting him from my mom. She'd take him to the city shelter, and he'd be gassed.

"You're not as innocent as you think," Nina chuckled. "If that invisible thingamajig on your forehead worked *all* the time, your parents would know about Raindrop by now. Besides," she added, "you won't have to lie. The bus will take you right to the corner of your street, and my mom really *is* in a hurry since she's got to get my dad from the airport."

"Okay, okay, I get it, but . . ."

"But what?"

"I've never been on the bus by myself," I admitted.

This time, Nina let out an impatient sigh. "Gosh, Windy. You're beginning to sound like Elena. I thought you were cooler than this. Look," she said, putting her hand on my shoulder, "taking the bus is no big deal. I do it all the time. It's so easy. You don't even have to transfer from here."

"But . . ."

"I tell you what. I'll wait till you get on. I'll even buy your ticket." She reached into her coin purse. I saw several bills in there, which surprised me since she'd already spent a lot of money.

"Here." She tried to give me a few dollars.

I waved it away. "Maybe I should call my parents."

She stepped back. "Call your parents? I thought you were my friend."

"I am. Didn't we just become breath sisters?"

"I *thought* so. But as soon as you call your parents, they'll call my mom, and we won't get to hang out anymore. She'll make me quit band, or worse, make me transfer to another school again. She's real strict, Windy. I'll probably spend the whole summer locked in my room."

This was horrible. I could feel Nina's trust slipping away.

So what if she snuck out and asked me to lie to my parents? She just wanted to spend time with me, right? I should be flattered, not mad. I imagined Nina looking out her window as the neighborhood kids walked to the pool or skated down her street. I imagined her phone ringing and her mom saying, "She can't talk. She's grounded." And I imagined her mom changing the computer password to keep Nina from emailing her friends.

"I won't call my parents," I decided. "I'll take the bus."

"It's okay, Windy. *I'm* the one who messed up, remember?"

"No, I'll take it. Really. It's no big deal. Like you said, it's one bus, no transfers."

"Are you sure?" Nina asked.

I nodded.

"At least let me buy the ticket," she said.

"You kind of *have* to," I teased, "since I don't have any more money."

As I took a few dollars, she hugged me.

"Windy, you're better than all the breath sisters I had at my other school."

The bus wasn't so bad, especially since none of the passengers noticed me. They all had the same blank stare. They smelled like fried chicken or hamburgers and wore uniforms with fast food logos. Or they wore cleaning lady aprons or the bright orange vests of construction workers. Everyone was getting off work, and they looked as tired as my mom. Some even fell asleep, yet they magically awoke at the right stops. I knew I was getting close to my neighborhood when I started to see Spanish billboards like the McDonald's sign with *"Me encanta"* below the golden arches and the Bank of America sign picturing a girl in cap and gown next to the words *"En cada marca de tu vida. Hablemos."*

Sure enough, I reached the corner of my street and got off. When I stepped through the front door, I found Dad leaning on the armrest of the sofa, a no-no in our house, while Mom stood with her hands on her hips. Something had upset her — something that kept her standing after a hard day of work. I touched my neck, worried she could see a mark there.

"Nina's mom was in a hurry," I quickly explained. "She said she'll meet you next time."

"It's just as well," Mom said. "Your father and I are having a discussion."

That was too easy, I thought. Usually, my folks had a zillion questions. Then again, "discussion" was their code word for "fight."

They didn't say anything else. They didn't move. I felt like the remote control button that had "paused" their scene.

"I guess I'll go to my room now," I said.

They nodded. I could tell they wanted some privacy.

As usual, all three cats were in my bedroom. It was their favorite spot in the afternoon when the sunlight poured in. I put my purse and Dillard's bag on my vanity, and Cloudy immediately went to investigate. El Niño barely turned his head to acknowledge me, but Sunny jumped on the bed, rolled onto his back, and purred. That was how he said, "Rub my belly, please."

"Later," I whispered to him because I wanted to eavesdrop on my parents. If they weren't mad at me, then what were they fighting about?

I stood at my door, hoping to overhear them, but my parents never yelled, even when they were *double* mad. So I tiptoed and stood behind the doorway that led to the living room.

"So you don't like my hair?" Dad asked Mom.

"No. It's too orange."

"It's supposed to be blond. Just give it a few days."

"Why would you change your hair color in the first place?"

"Because the people at the TV station prefer light hair."

"But you're not on TV," Mom said. "You work at the radio station. So it doesn't matter what you look like."

"I might work at the radio station *now*, but being on TV has always been my dream. No one listens to the radio anymore."

"That's not true," Mom said. "Lots of people listen."

"Lots *more* watch TV."

I heard Mom sigh. I recognized that sigh. It meant the hard truth would follow.

"Listen, Alfonso, you have to face it," she said. "You didn't get the job. You need to accept it and move on."

"Do you think my parents accepted their situation?" Dad asked. "Why do you think they left Mexico? Why do you think they worked so hard?" He paused, then answered his own question. "They wanted me to live the American dream. And this is it. Being on TV. And I can be on TV if I . . . if I . . ."

"If you what?" Mom asked.

"If I look the part," he said.

"There are all kinds of people on TV," Mom told him. "White, black, brown."

"And all of them change their hair and their clothes — whatever it takes."

"Changing your looks won't get you that job. A lot more goes into being a TV weatherman."

I heard my dad stand up. "Are you saying I don't know my stuff?" He sounded seriously offended. "Because I'm better than that guy they hired."

He stomped away before Mom could answer. He probably went to the garage. Whenever he felt frustrated, he calmed himself by reorganizing his tools. He'd probably reorganize his tools *and* sweep the cobwebs today.

Before I could sneak back to my room, Mom discovered me.

"What are you doing here, Windy?"

"I was on my way to the bathroom," I said.

"No, you weren't. You were eavesdropping."

The truth-marquee on my forehead must have been working again.

"Have you figured out an interest?" she asked. "Because summer's right around the corner." She didn't care about my interests — not right now anyway. She just wanted to scold me because she was mad at Dad, which meant she was mad at everyone.

"I like cats," I offered.

"Cats?" I could tell she wanted to explode with impatience. "Well, go figure out how to make them useful. All those things do is eat, sleep, and leave hairballs on the floor."

With that, she marched to her bedroom.

So I went back to my own room, kicked off my shoes, and plopped on the bed. Cloudy, always the investigator, jumped off the vanity to sniff my shoes. He sniffed them for a long time, as if he could smell all the stores I'd walked through.

"You nutty cat," I teased.

I'd had a tough day. Raindrop, my parents, Mrs. Vargas, the choking game. I opened my notebook and added a new list — "The Top Five Things to Worry About."

CHAPTER 10

Necktie Challenge

*I*n San Antonio, a light rain can cause a dozen car accidents, while a heavy rain can wash away swing sets and whole trucks. But even after the worst storms, the sun returns, sometimes with a rainbow, and the city looks as if it had a good scrubbing behind the ears. I always go outside and wonder what all the fuss was about — why the storm seemed scarier than it actually was. That's how I felt about the choking game. I'd spent a whole Sunday worried about it, but when I walked onto campus, I remembered that Nina and I were breath sisters now, and this secret made me feel special. After all, the other girls didn't know about the choking game, so they didn't have a breath sister like me.

That morning, I got to school early as usual and waited where the buses dropped off kids. Elena's bus was always the first to arrive, and she was always the first to exit.

"You're like a human cargo ship," I said as I grabbed her gym bag and her piccolo case. She had tennis shoes slung over her shoulder, a Target bag filled with fresh school supplies, and a suitcase with wheels for her books. "You must be the only person who empties her whole locker each weekend."

"I can't help it," Elena admitted. "Two days is a long time. I might get bored. I might want to review something."

"Then take *one* book, not *all* of them."

"But what if I'm not in the mood for that book? If I take all of them, I'm bound to find at least one that's interesting to read."

"So which one was interesting this time?" I asked.

Elena giggled. "I don't know. I never got bored enough to find out."

Elena's locker was on the second floor, so we lugged her books up the stairs. She pulled the suitcase while I pushed it, the wheels as wobbly as those on old shopping carts. Then Elena's tennis shoes slipped from her shoulder, and the Target bag tore, so we had to chase the pencils that fell out. We restocked her locker, both of us digging our shoulders into the door to close it. We still had fifteen minutes before classes began, so we went to the restroom to kill time. "Did you and Nina have fun at the mall?" Elena asked.

"It was okay," I said. Part of me wanted to tell her about the choking game, but when I imagined myself telling her, I also imagined Elena lecturing me about how dumb it was. There was no way she could understand what being a breath sister meant. Plus, I'd promised Nina to keep it a secret. Somehow keeping this a secret felt like lying, but how could it be lying if I wasn't saying anything? I had to keep my promise, so I wouldn't mention the choking game. "Look what Nina got me," I said instead as I reached into my purse and pulled out the scarf. "Nina got one, too. We're going to wear them on the same day."

"Where did you buy it? I'll need one, too."

Why was Elena such a copycat? Sometimes she really got on my nerves. "I don't remember," I lied. "We went to so many stores." She looked down, disappointed. "But look what else I got." I took out the compact, mascara, and lip gloss. "Want some?"

"No, I'm not into makeup, and neither are you."

"Yes, I am."

"Since when?"

"Since now."

She rolled her eyes. I could tell she didn't believe me. See? That was why I couldn't mention the choking game, because Elena could be — what did she call it? — a bummefier, as in someone who makes things a bummer. I thought about the times she talked me out of toilet papering Courtney's house, or sneaking into a theater to see an R-rated horror flick, or keeping twenty bucks from a wallet we found at the library one day. I knew these things were wrong, but they were fun, too. And none of them really hurt anyone. If I always listened to Elena, Raindrop would have starved by now. I wasn't going to let her talk me out of makeup, too, so I rubbed the compact powder on my face and then applied the lip gloss and mascara.

"How do I look?" I asked.

"Like Windy — only with shinier lips and clumpy eyelashes," she teased. "I don't see why you wear makeup when your glasses hide it all."

I looked in the mirror. With my glasses, I hardly noticed the mascara. Elena was right. Why wear makeup when I wore glasses, too? After all, no one would notice. Ronnie wouldn't notice. Then again, I didn't *need* my glasses, did I? True, my vision was blurry and I couldn't see the chalkboards without them, but I could see large objects like my classroom doors. I could probably find my desk, too.

I moved my lenses up and down, trying to compare how I looked.

"That settles it," I said. "No glasses. I can always put them on when the teacher writes on the board."

"I was kidding," Elena laughed. "Don't take them off. You'll get lost."

I ignored her, folded my glasses, and slipped them into my purse.

"Just point out my locker, will you?" I said. "I know which section it's in, but I can't read the numbers very well."

"Do you need me to unlock your combination, too?" she asked.

"Good idea. Otherwise, I won't be able to get my books."

Elena shook her head, but she walked me to my locker and opened it anyway.

Then I went to my morning classes. Nina was a no-show, so nothing exciting happened — except that Liz asked where she was. She asked *me.* That was when I realized that she wasn't spending much time with Courtney and Alicia anymore. She was doing her own thing, with her own group of in-crowd girls, and all of them were wearing scarves like Nina.

Without my glasses, I couldn't see the video in science, but I could hear just fine. And since I was forced to listen closely, I took more notes. I probably learned more about Isaac Newton than anyone else in class — like, he's the guy who came up with gravity, not the guy who invented Fig Newtons. See how smart I was getting? I should have ditched my glasses long ago.

Finally, it was lunchtime.

"Can you read that again?" I asked Elena as we stood in line. Each day the cafeteria ladies wrote the menu on a chalkboard.

"Quit being so helpless," she said. "If you're not going to wear your glasses, you'll have to depend on your other senses — you know, learn to be more *nose*pendent or *ear*pendent."

"Hey, guys." It was Nina.

"Where were you?" I asked. "We thought you were absent."

"I had a really bad headache," she said, "so I spent the morning in the nurse's office. She let me sleep it off."

"Is that why your eyes are bloodshot?" Elena asked.

I punched her. She could be so nosy.

Luckily, Nina didn't mind explaining. "Yeah. Sometimes I have high blood pressure, and it makes the little vessels burst. That's what causes my headaches, too."

I winced. The whole thing sounded painful.

Today, her scarf was blue silk with a gold paisley pattern. She wore it like a necktie and stroked it absentmindedly as we waited in line.

"You're here," I heard Ronnie say.

"Yes," I answered. "After speech, I got here as fast as I could."

He laughed. "Not you, Trouper. I meant Nina." Then turning to her, he said, "Didn't see you in class today."

"Major headache," she said.

"Are you feeling better now?" He sounded really concerned. Why was he so concerned?

"Oh, yeah. I'm fine. I just get headaches sometimes. It's no big deal."

She seemed tired. If I remembered correctly, she'd had a headache last week, too, but not one that sent her to the nurse.

The line inched forward, but we were still twelve or fifteen people from the serving ladies.

"So, Ronnie," I said, hoping to jump-start the conversation, "how was your weekend?"

Before he could answer, Elena said, "We saw Windy's adopt-a-granny!"

I wanted to pinch her. Why'd she tell him I spent time with a fake grandma?

"Your adopt-a-what?" he asked.

"Just a lady we helped out," Nina said, saving me from my embarrassing moment. "We did some volunteer work at an old folks' home, and then Windy and I went to the mall."

"Wow. You girls are really nice to help the old people. I have to help my *abuelita* all the time."

How cool was that? Ronnie and I both called our grandmas "*abuelita*."

"Old people have trouble walking," he went on. "And they forget all sorts of things — like their own names."

True, a lot of people at Pleasant Hill had wheelchairs or walked with canes, but a lot of them went to the exercise room for aerobics. And even though Mr. Dawson had a bad knee, his wife, Mrs. Dawson, ran the marathon last year. We took a field trip to the Alamodome to cheer as she crossed the finish line. And, yes, I did have to introduce myself to some of the residents each time I saw them, but Mrs. Vargas *never* forgot my name. She remembered all our conversations, too, and since she could summarize a whole week's worth of soap operas, she must have a great memory. I wanted to tell Ronnie the truth about my friends, but even though I wasn't part of the in-crowd — not yet, anyway — I knew it wasn't cool to correct a really cute guy.

"It was Windy's idea," Nina said about going to Pleasant Hill. "She likes to help old people."

"And cats," Elena added.

"That's really nice," Ronnie said again. "Old people and cats — they have a lot in common."

I nodded even though I didn't know what he meant.

"So did you buy anything at the mall?" he asked.

"Of course," Nina said. "Haven't you noticed something different about Windy?"

Ronnie studied me and scratched his chin. "Hey," he finally realized, "you lost your glasses."

"Well, kind of," I said.

"Are you wearing contacts or something?"

"No, I mean, I . . ."

"I never noticed this before," he went on, "but your eyes are really brown. They're as brown as . . . as . . . as brown as the eyes on a horse."

I blushed. Horses were beautiful, right?

"And . . ." he pondered.

"And?" I said, hopeful.

"And . . . your eyes are . . . they're . . . squinty!"

"Squinty?"

"Yeah, like the eyes of . . . the eyes of . . . of another brown-eyed, squinty horse."

Elena burst out laughing. This time, I *did* pinch her. Luckily, Nina saved me again.

"That's so sweet of you, Ronnie. Maybe you could meet us at the mall next time. We could all go shopping together."

"Really?" he said. "That would be cool."

"And I'll go, too," Elena said.

Secretly, I didn't want Elena, or even Nina, in the picture. Just Ronnie. We'd sit at the food court or go into a photography booth and make silly faces as the camera flashed our picture. Then he'd buy me a gift, probably something small since he didn't have a job — a flower or coin purse or teddy bear that fit in my pocket. Then we . . .

Nina nudged me, bringing me back to reality. The line inched forward again as we finally reached the serving ladies.

"Well, I'm off," Ronnie said.

"Aren't you going to eat?" I asked.

"You mean *that* greasy stuff? No way. It'll kill you. That's why I go to the vending machines."

I watched him walk away. Without my glasses, he was a blur in no time.

When he was out of earshot, Elena said, "Windy, I'm going to say this straight. Ronnie's cute, but he's dense."

"No, he's not," I blurted.

"How can you deny it? He thinks the vending machines are healthier than the hot line, and he just compared you to a horse."

"You can't blame him for trying to be poetic," Nina said. "Maybe his words don't come out right, but at least he sees the best in people."

"Yeah," I added. "Don't be so hard on him, Elena."

Elena glanced at me and then at Nina. I knew that look. She had a comeback, one that would hit me like a bucket of cold water. I waited for it, but it never came. Maybe she felt outnumbered. Maybe she was too hungry to insist on the last word. Or maybe, just maybe, when she saw Nina and me, maybe she realized we were breath sisters now. Whatever the reason, Elena swallowed her comeback and turned away.

CHAPTER 11

Blackout Game

Thursday started on a good note. Nina and I agreed to wear our new scarves, so everyone would know that we were friends. Plus, Mom gave me twenty dollars for the book fair. Mrs. Campos planned to take the class, so even though Mom ordered me to buy a book that would help me discover my interest, I was glad about the chance to skip speech.

As our class filed into the book fair, the librarian greeted us, and even without my glasses, I could see the bright ABC's sewn on her denim vest. A few vendors had set up tables with books, stationery, erasers, cutesy pens, and key chains, and a library assistant manned the Book Swap table where students could trade "gently read" books. Each year, the librarian sponsored a contest and invited us to make dioramas or presentation boards featuring our favorite books. The best entries were showcased on a horseshoe arrangement of tables called Reader's Row. I could vaguely see it at the far end of the library. The contest winners got a ten dollar gift certificate to the Twig Bookshop, and all participants got extra credit in their English class. I should have entered since I had a C, but that was the problem with extra credit. The kids who really needed it never bothered. Of course, Elena didn't need extra credit. How could you bump up an A? But she'd entered the contest anyway.

"I can't wait to show you my project," she told Nina and me.

Two other classes were already in the library, so the teachers ordered us to sit down. We'd have to browse in shifts.

"Who's that waving at us?" I asked, squinting to see better.

"It's Liz," Nina said. "She wants us to sit at her table."

Even though Liz had been saying hello lately, she'd never asked me to sit with her. So I felt surprised until I remembered that I was wearing a yellow scarf, just like Nina. Liz had a scarf, too, white with pink swirls.

As soon as we sat down, Liz said to me, "Your new contacts look great."

"She's not wearing contacts," Elena explained. "She got rid of her glasses because she's boycentric now."

"Boycentric?"

I gently kicked Elena to keep her from defining her latest word-morph. Luckily, she got the hint. I knew she didn't mean to embarrass me, but still . . . why couldn't she be cool?

"Can you see?" Liz asked.

"Sure," I said. "Turns out I didn't need my glasses after all."

"Your vision got better?"

"Kind of. I mean, not really. I mean . . ."

"She ate a lot of carrots," Nina said. "Carrots are really good for eyesight."

Just then, Ronnie showed up and took the chair beside me. There was another empty chair, but he picked this one, with me to his left.

"Where were you?" Nina asked him. She was sitting on his right.

"Looking around. They got some cool stuff for sale. Check it out."

He opened his hand and revealed two bracelets. One was a braid of green, gold, and red, while the other was a braid of blue, pink, and yellow.

"Those are real pretty," Liz said.

"Yeah," Ronnie agreed. "I couldn't decide which one to buy, so I got both." He placed them on the table. "Which one do you like?" he asked Nina.

"I'm not sure. What do you think, Windy?"

"I like the one with blue because it reminds me of Raindrop's eyes."

"Then I like the one with green," she said.

"Take it. It's yours," Ronnie offered.

Suddenly my stomach twisted up. Why was he giving her a bracelet? What about the rest of us? There were three other girls at the table.

Nina glanced at me. She knew I liked him, so she pushed the bracelet aside. "That's really nice, but I can't."

"Sure you can. It's a get-well gift," Ronnie said. "For that headache you had, remember?"

"You *were* feeling bad," Elena said.

"Then it's settled." Ronnie slid the bracelet back to Nina, and then he turned to me. "You can have the one with blue, since you like it so much."

He placed it in my hand, and as he did so, I felt the heat of *his* hand. My jealous stomach relaxed as I imagined slow dancing with him, how warm he'd be. Elena was right. I was getting boycentric. But I couldn't help myself. For the first time, a really cute guy had noticed me. When I analyzed the situation, I realized that Ronnie really bought the bracelet for me. Sure, he paid for two — but probably because he didn't want the other girls to hate me. Maybe he didn't have enough money to buy one for everybody. Choosing to give the extra to Nina made total sense because he could use her headache as an excuse. But he didn't need an excuse to give *me* a bracelet. He gave it to me because . . . because he *liked* me. That *had* to be the reason.

I put it on. The blue, pink, and yellow braid was very pretty. "Thank you," I said.

"Hey, look." Nina held out her own wrist. "We're like twin sisters now." She winked because we *were* sisters — breath sisters.

"You have the same scarves, too," Ronnie noticed.

"I'm going to buy mine this weekend," Elena said, "so we can *all* match."

Nina turned to Liz and mouthed, "Whatever," and Liz chuckled a little. Luckily, I was the only one who noticed. For a split second, I felt sorry for Elena. Then I got annoyed. Why did she want to be like us? Why couldn't she be her own person?

Just then, I heard some jostling behind me and discovered Courtney and Alicia making their way to our table.

"Hi, Liz. Hi, Ronnie," they said, ignoring the rest of us.

Nina turned to me and rolled her eyes. I rolled my eyes, too. Those girls were so immature. I couldn't believe they still blamed Nina for the day no one clapped.

"We've got room over there," Alicia said, nodding to an empty table near the reference desk. "You don't *have* to sit here if you don't want."

"Yeah," Courtney added. "Come join us."

"Maybe later," Liz said.

They glanced at Ronnie.

"Ditto," he said.

Courtney and Alicia stood there, like two actresses who'd forgotten their lines. For a moment, I felt sorry for them because I knew how it felt to be ignored — like the time I needed a partner in science. Everyone had paired up but me. I felt like such a leftover. Then Pimple Jim walked in, so I had to work with him. And to make things worse, *he* complained about being stuck with *me* even though I was in the GP, a whole step above his out-crowd status.

I didn't like to be on the mean side of things, even if it meant I was cool, but then Courtney told Liz, "If that's how you're going to be, don't expect a seat at our lunch table." And even though she wasn't addressing me, I felt offended.

"Whatever," Liz said with the famous *W* sign.

Alicia made the *W* sign with both hands, then pointed at Liz, her way of saying, "Double 'whatever' to *you*."

Courtney just flicked her hair and turned away.

As soon as they reached their table, Nina laughed. Loud. Courtney and Alicia glanced back, and their paranoid expressions made our whole table laugh. Mrs. Campos had to tap the lectern to hush us.

Then she said, "If you haven't looked around, please do so now."

Elena and I stood up.

"Aren't you coming?" we asked Liz and Nina.

Liz said, "I don't like to read."

And Nina said, "My mom never gives me extra cash."

"Really?" I wondered out loud. "She gave you a lot for the mall last week."

Nina looked away, taking a moment to answer. "She made an exception that day," she explained, "since I was volunteering at the old folks' home."

"You weren't volunteering," Elena said.

"According to my mom, I was." Nina's voice was stern. She meant to end the conversation. I could tell she was a little upset, and I couldn't blame her. Sometimes, Elena didn't know when to keep her mouth shut.

"Besides," Nina added, glancing at Liz, "don't we have to go to the restroom?"

Liz said, "Oh, yeah, that's right. It's an emergency."

"A *serious* emergency," Nina said. Then she turned to me. "Didn't you say you had to go, too?"

I didn't remember saying that, but I noticed that Nina was fiddling with her scarf. Was this a secret breath sister code?

"I better go, too," I said, and before she could protest, I told Elena, "I'll hurry back to see your project, okay?"

"Okay. I guess I can look at the books first." She sounded seriously disappointed, so I promised myself to get back soon.

"Will you watch our stuff?" Nina asked Ronnie.

"Sure," he said.

Elena headed toward the books, while I followed Nina and Liz to the restroom. As soon as we got there, Liz said, "Nina told me about the mall. I think it's so cool that you're a breath sister."

"You told her about the mall?" I asked Nina. "I thought it was a secret."

"It is," Nina said, "but breath sisters don't keep secrets from each other — just from the people who aren't part of our group."

I stood silent for a while as I tried to work out this puzzle.

"Are you saying Liz is your breath sister, too?"

"*Our* breath sister," Nina corrected. "And not only Liz but every girl who wears a scarf." I must have looked disappointed because she said, "Just think about all the new friends you have."

"That's right." Liz laughed. "Don't you like hanging out with me?"

"Of course, I do," I rushed to say. The last thing I needed was to insult my new friends. "I'm just surprised, that's all."

"Well, don't be," Liz said. "Everybody thinks you're so cool." She put her hand on my shoulder and squeezed lightly. Then she went to the door and peeked out. "The coast is clear."

"Okay. So who wants to go first?" Nina asked.

"For what?" I wanted to know.

"The choking game. Why do you think we're here?"

"I don't know. I thought we had to use the restroom."

They cracked up, told me I was hilarious, but since I wasn't trying to be funny, I felt a little offended. Thank goodness, they calmed down. I didn't like being laughed at.

Nina turned to me. "Why don't you go first, Windy? And this time, don't tap out."

"But I'll faint."

They laughed again. What was so funny? Was I really that ridiculous?

"That's the whole point," Liz explained.

"I know," I said even though fainting seemed like the stupidest idea in the world. How could it possibly be fun? I remembered how I saw green dots last Saturday, how the walls closed in, how the pressure hurt my head. I had been terrified. No way was I playing the choking game again. But Liz and Nina thought it was fun. They expected me to play. I could tell that our friendship depended on it. How did I get myself into this situation? I really wanted to be part of the in-crowd. I wanted it as much as I *didn't* want to play the choking game.

"I'll have to play next time," I said as I backed out of the restroom, "because I promised Elena I'd hurry back. Plus, my mom expects me to buy something."

"Are you sure?" Nina said.

"Yeah. Next time, I'll play. I won't tap out. I promise. But if I don't hurry back now, Elena will send over a search team."

They laughed. "That sounds like something she'd do," I heard Liz say.

When I got back to the hallway, I took a deep breath, relieved. I managed to escape this time, but what about the next?

As I stepped into the library, I saw several in-crowd girls with scarves. That meant they were playing, too, didn't it? They probably didn't tap out. They must be fainting on a regular basis, yet they seemed fine. Maybe I was making a big deal out of nothing. Maybe the choking game wasn't as bad as I thought.

I wanted to talk to Elena about it, but when I found her, she was waiting impatiently at Reader's Row. There was no way she would ever understand. Elena knew a lot about books and numbers and science, but nothing about having cool friends.

When I reached her, she grabbed my elbow. We didn't even glance at the other contest entries. Elena had designed a presentation board *and* a diorama, and even though she didn't win first place, her project was very impressive.

"I read *A Skating Life: My Story*," she said. "It's by Dorothy Hamill. She won gold in the 1976 Olympics, when our parents were just little kids."

The presentation board had a summary of the book and pictures of Dorothy Hamill. Elena also included a chart with the gold, silver, and bronze winners of every Olympic skater since. The diorama featured an ice-skater twirling on one toe.

"Remember that old jewelry box I used to have?" Elena said.

I nodded.

"I took it apart. This is the ballerina that was inside it. I painted her ballet shoes white and used aluminum to make little blades."

"And you used layers of white tissue paper to make the ice," I said.

"That's right. I wish the ballerina still twirled, but the little motor in the jewelry box broke a long time ago."

"It still looks great. How do you come up with these ideas?"

"I don't know. I'm always finding ways to combine things, even if they don't seem to go together at first. Like a jewelry box and a skating rink. Who knew they had something in common?"

I remembered Ronnie's comment the other day, about cats and old people having so much in common. I still didn't know what he meant, but I didn't want to ask him. He'd think I was *double* dense for not figuring it out.

"You know why I like ice-skating so much?" Elena asked.

"I always wondered," I said, "especially because you don't even own a pair of skates."

"Well, I don't *really* want to go to the Olympics. Those girls start skating when they're four. But I love to watch them. They have to be athletic, but they have to be creative, too. When they do their routines, they tell a story. And it doesn't matter what language they speak, because they don't use words. They use movement. So their message reaches the whole world."

I nodded. Elena might look and act like a little girl, but sometimes she was as wise as a ninety-year-old.

After she straightened up her display, we looked at a few other entries — a book about the assassination of Abraham Lincoln presented as a graphic novel and a diorama of whales that included a sound track of their songs. We then made our way to the vendors, and spent some time looking at bookmarks.

"Liz and Nina just got back," Elena said.

I looked toward our table but I couldn't see so well without my glasses.

"Liz looks a little pale," Elena added.

Suddenly, I wanted to protect Liz and our choking game secret. "Really? She looks normal to me."

"I guess," Elena said.

I was running out of time, so I skipped the fiction and

poetry books, figuring I'd find an interest in the nonfiction section.

Pilates? No. Photography? No. Dinosaurs, galaxies, diseases, pyramids, cars? No, no, no to everything. Meanwhile, Elena had picked up a paranormal mystery, a cookie recipe book, and a poster of cute panda bears.

"Can I help you find something?" the saleslady asked.

"Do you have anything about cats?"

She showed me a book about housetraining cats, one about different breeds of cats, and a silly novel called *The Cat Who Saved the Planet Earth*. I shook my head to all of them.

"How about this?" The saleslady handed me a book called *Careers for Animals*.

"No," I said. "I don't want to be a vet or animal trainer."

"This isn't about careers *with* animals. It's about different jobs that they can do. Like seeing-eye dogs. I'm sure it has a section about cats, too."

Now *that* sounded interesting. I giggled as I imagined El Niño, Sunny, and Cloudy taking the bus to work every morning.

"I'll take it," I said. Since I had extra money, I added a crafting book for Mrs. Vargas. Sometimes she and her friends did projects together, and I thought the book might give them new ideas.

"Five minutes," Mrs. Campos announced. "Complete your purchases and return to your tables. I'll dismiss you when the bell rings."

When Elena and I got to our table, I gasped. I thought I'd black out from the panic. Nina was showing Liz and Ronnie my TOP FIVE notebook! It wasn't exactly a secret since I often shared my notebook with friends, but some of my lists were private. And some were kind of insulting. Last night, I'd written a list called "The Top Five Things I'm Glad I Can't See Anymore" and the number one thing was armpit sweat stains. Lots of my classmates had armpit sweat stains. They'd hate me if they saw what I wrote. But worse than that, I had lists about Ronnie and Nina in there. I even had lists about my problems!

"Give that back!" I cried. "It's private."

"Don't worry," Nina said. "I'd never show your secret entries. I only showed the ones we wrote at the mall."

"She's telling the truth," Liz said. "You guys wrote some funny lists."

"Yeah," Ronnie agreed. "I like the one about gross stuff under the fingernails." They laughed remembering it, and I felt my anger dissolve when Ronnie said, "You've got a great sense of humor, Trouper."

"Windy's got a superific sense of humor," Elena said. "In fact, *we've* written some funny lists, too." She took the notebook. "Can I show them?"

I shrugged. "I guess it's okay. As long as you show only the lists we wrote together."

"Of course," Elena said.

She flipped through the pages, pausing to read the titles, then flipping through *more* pages. I'd been writing a lot lately, so she had to go way back. Finally, she stopped. Her eyes scanned the page. She was smiling, but then she shook her head as if to clear her thoughts. She read on and clamped her lips. I'd been her friend for many, many years, so I could tell that something had upset her.

"What's wrong?" I asked.

She gave me the notebook and pointed to the title. "The Top Five Reasons Elena is a Nerd."

"Why are you upset about that? We wrote it together, remember?"

"But we didn't *finish* it together," she said.

That was right. My mom had come home and interrupted us. We never got to the number one reason Elena was a nerd. But there it was: "The number one reason Elena is a nerd is because she makes up stupid words, which makes her a . . ." I saw three lines of scribbles and cross-outs as if someone were trying to create a word-morph that described Elena. Finally, the mystery author wrote, "mega-nerd."

"I didn't write this," I said.

"I know. That's not your handwriting. But this notebook is always with you, which makes you an accessory."

"That's silly," Nina laughed. "What's a purse got to do with it?"

"Not a purse," Elena said. "But you wouldn't know the other definition of 'accessory,' would you? Because you get all your vocabulary from a *thick*tionary, which is a dictionary for people who are thick in the head!"

I couldn't believe she talked back to Nina. Elena was never rude. Then, I thought about the last few days, the times I took Nina's side or chose to hang out with her instead. I thought about the comebacks Elena had held back.

Nina looked at me and said, "Is that the kind of person you want as a friend?"

I didn't know what she meant. Was she talking about Elena's looks, her habits, or the way she sassed back? And what kind of person *did* I want as a friend? What were friends for, anyway? Weren't they supposed to help you? Nina had helped me, several times, but Elena had always helped me, too.

"Say something," Elena begged.

I couldn't. I was still muddling through all my questions.

Elena grabbed her things. "Are you coming?" she asked, and I knew she wanted me to make a choice. But I couldn't. I stood there like a lost child at the mall.

"Fine," Elena said as she headed out. Just then, the dismissal bell rang and a dozen students filled the space between us.

I glanced at the notebook again, recognizing the handwriting.

"When did you write this?" I asked Nina.

"When we were at the food court, remember? I told you I finished some of your lists."

"You should have told me *which* lists. I would have erased this. Now I'm in trouble with Elena."

"She'll get over it."

"No, she won't," I said, my voice cracking a bit.

How could Nina make fun of the word-morphs? Elena loved them as much as I loved my lists. That's how we expressed ourselves. Sure, it was nerdy, but we never cared. Sometimes the perfect word or list could make our frustrations melt away.

Ronnie said, "Maybe you can apologize."

I couldn't tell if he wanted me to apologize to Elena or if he wanted Nina to apologize to me. I guess Nina couldn't tell, either, because she got defensive.

"Don't you see what Elena's doing?" she told me. "She's making you feel bad when *she's* the one who can't take a joke."

"Yeah," Liz said. "People always make jokes."

She loosened her scarf a bit. Her neck looked red from the choking game. I hadn't wanted to play, yet I hated to know that Liz and Nina had played without me.

"Don't you and Elena make fun of people, too?" Nina asked.

She had a point. We made fun of people all the time — but we made fun of people we didn't like. So did this mean Nina didn't like Elena?

"Time to go," the librarian said. "We've got other classes coming soon."

"Come on. I'm starved," Liz said, grabbing her purse.

"Me, too," Ronnie said.

I followed them out. They were already talking about something else. But I wasn't finished. I didn't know what I wanted to say or how to say it — only that I *should* speak, that I would speak if I were braver. I felt guilty, ashamed, indignant, jealous, frustrated, impatient, regretful, and betrayed. I was a rainbow of emotion — not only because rainbows were beautiful and colorful — but because they had bands that blended into each other and edges that I could never quite see.

We reached the cafeteria. I put my glasses on and scanned the room. Elena wasn't there. I took my glasses off again and sat at a table with Nina, Liz, Ronnie, and a few in-crowd kids who'd abandoned Courtney and Alicia, but even with all those people around, I felt lonely.

CHAPTER 12

Trip to Heaven

*E*lena wouldn't take my calls, wouldn't give me a chance to apologize. So the next morning, I decided to wait for Nina's bus instead, but she was absent again. And walking through the school by myself felt as awkward as writing my name with the wrong hand.

"Hey, Windy," I heard Liz say. "Where's Nina?" She and a few other in-crowd girls waited for my answer. "We figured you'd know what's going on."

"Oh, yeah," I lied. "Nina and I talk on the phone all the time. She got a bad headache this morning, but it's nothing serious. She'll be back next week."

"Tell me about it," Liz said. "I had a headache last night, too."

A few other girls nodded. I guessed headaches were contagious now.

I walked with them. Hanging out with someone other than Elena or Nina felt strange and unreal, like when I dreamed I was on a trip to heaven, looking down at all the people crying over me. Only now I was alive and well. Only this *wasn't* a dream.

How mag-tastic — I mean, great — this was! Finally, being with the popular girls. And they were so nice, so welcoming — except for Courtney and Alicia. When they saw me walking with their friends, they blocked our way, crossed their arms, and said, "What's this?"

I thought Liz and the girls would disown me, but instead, they flashed the "whatever" sign. Then we all walked around Courtney and Alicia as if they were cars parked in our way.

A little later, one of the girls said, "Those two are so stuck-up."

"Yeah," the others replied. "They can be mean, too."

"And those headbands are so lame," the first girl added. "Can't they see no one wears them anymore?"

We all giggled.

"I guess they didn't get the memo," I said, which prompted Liz to give me a high five.

"I bet they don't know anything about the choking game," someone added.

"Even if they do," Liz said, "they'd be too chicken to play."

Everyone laughed again before moving on to other topics. As the girls chatted about the upcoming weekend, I thought about how sneaky transformations could be. Even though the floor in the main hallway had the same black and red checkered tile, and the creepy portrait of Horace Mann hung in the exact same spot since forever, the building somehow felt different — as if the school had both changed and stayed the same. Like the seasons of San Antonio. Spring and summer were hot, while fall and winter were not-so-hot, and the only way you could tell the difference was by looking at the trees — one day full of leaves — the next day, completely bare. And when they were bare, it seemed as if they'd always been that way, as if the idea of leaves — like the idea of school without Nina or my new in-crowd friends — were impossible.

I missed Elena, but maybe our "breakup" was a good thing. Maybe she'd been holding me back. After all, she *did* look like an elementary school kid, and she *did* invent silly words. Plus, she excelled at everything. How could I enjoy my rare B's when Elena waved her A's in my face? No wonder

Courtney and Alicia turned on us after seeing Elena's Girl Scout sash with more achievement patches than we could count. It would've taken us years to catch up. Then I thought about all the useful advice Nina had given me this past month — about makeup, boys, and friendship. But what did Elena know? She just echoed my mom. *Don't feed that new cat. Don't wear makeup. Find an interest. Do your homework.* Elena was like a pesky sheepdog, always yapping and telling me which way to go.

The more I thought about it, the more I wondered how we'd stayed friends all this time.

My first three classes went okay. Then it was time for speech. On Fridays, Mrs. Campos took it easy. On the chalkboard, she wrote which chapter to read and which questions to answer. I always messed up my speeches, so I liked these easy grades. I needed them. Only today, I couldn't see the board.

I tapped Elena's shoulder. She didn't turn around.

"Hey, Elena," I whispered. "What does the board say?"

She shrugged. I couldn't believe it! She could see the board just fine because she'd already opened her book. Why hold such a grudge? It wasn't my fault she was still in the GP.

Fine then, I thought to myself. The pencil sharpener was next to the board. I walked up, sharpened my pencil, and memorized the instructions.

When I got to my desk, I quickly scribbled the questions I needed to answer — numbers 1, 4, 5, 7, 9 — 7, 9, and . . . I stalled. There were ten questions, but my mind couldn't hold all the numbers. No big deal. I went to Mrs. Campos's desk, grabbed a tissue, and pretended to blow my nose while I studied the last numbers. Then I hurried to my desk to write them down. But now I couldn't remember the page. Was it 231 or 213? I checked my book. There were questions on both pages. I tried to peek over Elena's shoulder, but she purposely blocked my view. This whole process was driving me nuts, and it was all her fault.

I couldn't sharpen my pencil again or get another tissue when I didn't have a runny nose. So I squinted really hard. I was so focused on deciphering the board that I didn't notice Mrs. Campos till she was right beside me.

"Can I see you outside for a moment?"

"Um, okay," I said nervously. She took students outside only when they were in trouble. I scanned my brain, but I couldn't figure out what I'd done wrong.

"Windy," Mrs. Campos began as we stepped into the hallway.

"Yes, ma'am?"

"Where are your glasses?"

"My glasses?"

She waited.

"I don't need them anymore." I knew what her next question would be, so I hurried to explain. "I'm not wearing contacts, if that's what you're wondering, and I didn't get that laser eye surgery. I just don't need glasses anymore."

"Is that so?" She scratched her head as if working through the most difficult puzzle. "Well," she decided, "you need them for *my* class, understand?"

I nodded.

"Starting today," she added.

"Today? I mean, I can't. I don't have them with me."

The glasses were in my purse, but the lie came so naturally, just like my lie about Nina earlier. For the first time, the truth-marquee on my forehead wasn't getting me in trouble.

"Okay, then," Mrs. Campos said. "But make sure you bring them Monday."

After trying to get the assignment and having a conference in the hallway, I couldn't answer more than six questions before the bell rang. What a double bummer! I needed every good grade I could get. I was so mad that I didn't bother to move aside so Elena could pass through the aisle. She didn't say, "Excuse me," or anything. She just turned around and looked for another escape route.

After she left, I grabbed my books and headed out.

"Wait up," Ronnie said as I made my way to the cafeteria.

"Oh, hi," I said, getting all nervous since he was walking with me. A lot of people probably noticed. This would definitely improve my standing with the in-crowd.

"I guess you're wondering why Mrs. Campos called me outside," I began. "It was nothing, really. She, um — she, well — she had a message for my mom, a secret message. I can't really tell you what it is, since it's a secret. But, hey, I'm wearing that bracelet you gave me yesterday. It's really pretty, see? I mean, it's beautiful. I've got lots of clothes that match it. But next time I go to the mall — maybe a whole bunch of us can go together? — anyway, next time, I'm going to look for a scarf that has these colors. Something real pretty — like the kind that Nina wears."

"Yeah, about Nina," he said, "I was wondering."

But I didn't let him finish. I was a car alarm that wouldn't shut off. "It's too bad Nina couldn't be here. She called this morning, so I could get her homework. She really wants to do well in school, but she gets these headaches, like the one she had the other day. High blood pressure and stuff. That's why her eyes are red sometimes."

"I was wondering —" Ronnie tried again.

But this time Liz interrupted. "I'll save you a seat at our lunch table," she told me.

I felt so astounded, so grateful, that I didn't hear what Ronnie said next.

"What did you say?" I asked.

"What are you doing after school?"

"Who? Me?"

He nodded.

"Nothing. Why?"

"Because I need to talk to you. In private. I want to ask you something."

Instead of a car with a haywire alarm, I was now a car with a dead battery. That's how dumfounded I felt. "You. Want. To. Ask. Me. Something?"

"Yeah. But I have to do my workout first. It takes about an hour."

"That's okay," I managed. "I'm going to the library for study hall. I can meet you in the gym when I'm finished."

"Cool," he said. He punched my shoulder playfully, then headed to the vending machine.

As we ate lunch, the in-crowd girls gossiped about the

Spanish teacher's date with the football coach and the counselor's face-lift last summer, but I kept thinking about Ronnie. What did he want to ask me? It had to be something romantic since he seemed nervous, since he said it was *private*. I desperately wished Nina were here. I didn't know the in-crowd girls well enough to ask for their advice, and Elena wouldn't know what to say even if we were speaking right now. But Nina was older and prettier. She probably had a lot of experience with boys. She'd tell me exactly how to act when Ronnie asked me his mysterious question.

So we were meeting after school. Did that mean he wanted to walk me home? I should take some books, see if he offered to carry them. Wasn't that what boyfriends did? Or maybe I should leave my books in my locker. After all, how was he supposed to hold my hand if he had a bunch of books in his arms? I couldn't believe he liked me! He was the cutest guy in school, and I — well — I wasn't the prettiest or most popular. But Ronnie was nice, the kind of guy who liked a girl for the person she was inside. That's what made him so special.

Since it was Friday, the library was nearly empty after school, but even though it was quiet, I couldn't concentrate. As I read a myth for my English class, Ronnie became the boy character, Pyramus, and I the girl character, Thisbe. We snuck out of our parents' houses just like the story said, but instead of dying and turning into mulberry bushes, we escaped to a faraway village and lived happily ever after. In science, I had to read about space exploration, and the Mars rovers turned into the human explorers, Ronnie and Windy. Even though we couldn't kiss through our space helmets, we fell in love because we were the only two on the planet. I tried to study history next. The chapter was about the Civil War, so I imagined being a nurse who took care of a wounded Ronnie. He fell in love with me because I didn't care about his missing leg.

What was wrong with me? I couldn't stop myself. With Ronnie on my mind, even math seemed romantic. After all, what was 1 + 1 if not the equation for love?

Study hall finally ended. I made my way to the gym. My stomach turned. My hands shook. The bones in my legs felt like strings of melting cheese. This was worse than giving a speech in the auditorium, in front of the whole school!

I got to the weightlifting room. The coaches welcomed everyone, but very few girls lifted weights. Mostly, football players and wrestlers used the equipment, or guys like Ronnie who liked to exercise but didn't want to compete on a team. I saw him gradually come into focus as he approached me.

"You're here," he said, sounding a little surprised even though he'd invited me. "Why don't you sit on this stool over here? I've got one more set. It'll only take a minute."

I took a seat as he went to the opposite wall where a mirror made the room seem larger than it really was. He sat on a bench, picked up something, and then lifted his right hand and waved. I waved back. He lifted his left hand and waved. So I waved back again. He waved at me two more times, alternating his hands. Was I supposed to alternate my hands, too?

When he returned to me, he said, "What are you doing?"

"Waving back."

"What? I'm not waving. I'm doing shoulder presses with the dumbbells. Didn't you see them in my hands?"

"Is that what you were holding?"

"Of course." He laughed a bit. "You need to tell the doctor that your new contacts aren't working."

I didn't bother to correct him about my eyes because I felt embarrassed about misinterpreting what I'd seen.

"I was going to work out some more," he said, "but I can take a break. I know you don't have all day."

He grabbed a towel, draped it around his neck, and told a few buddies that he'd be back.

"You live close by, don't you?" he asked.

"Yeah, a few streets away."

"Great. I'll walk with you."

So he *was* walking me home. How sweet! I waited for him to take my books, but he never offered, probably because he was sweaty from the workout.

We didn't say anything. Earlier I couldn't stop blabbering, but now I couldn't speak. Why did love bring out these extremes?

"So, Trouper," he finally said. "I can trust you, right?"

"Sure," I said.

"I mean, you're a good, honest person. You'd let me know, right, if I were about to make a fool of myself."

"You're not a fool," I rushed to say, realizing he was shy about his feelings.

"How can you be so sure?"

"Because I know what you want to talk about. I'm very observant. I can read the signs."

"There are signs?"

"Of course," I said, playfully bumping into him. "The bracelet. The compliments. The way you're always hanging around. Sometimes you even stand in the same lunch line even though you aren't going to buy any food."

"I guess the whole world has noticed, huh?"

He sounded so cute when he was embarrassed.

Then he said, "So that means Nina knows how I feel, right?"

I remembered all the boy advice she gave me. She probably knew better than anyone. "Of course," I said.

He sighed as if releasing the weight of the heaviest dumbbells.

"You don't know how relieved I am," he said. "To finally get this out in the open."

I never knew a smile could take over the whole body. Even my toes tingled with joy. "I know," I said. "I hate holding back, too."

"So you think I have a chance?"

"You *definitely* have a chance."

"Really?" he said. "Because I didn't think so."

"Why not?"

"Because Nina's so pretty and smart and — and — sophisticated! She could be with any guy she wants. Why would she like me when she's the prettiest girl in school?" I felt the smile in my body turn downward. Ronnie squeezed my shoulder and said, "Don't frown, Trouper. You're pretty, too."

"Yeah, I'm pretty," I repeated like a mindless robot.

"So you'll talk to her? Tell her what's up? And then report back to me?"

"Sure. No problem."

"I knew I could count on you," he said. Then he gave me a hug, like the kind my cousins give when I see them at barbecues. "Got to go," he said, turning back to school. We hadn't even reached my house yet!

I was so stupid, the stupidest girl in the world. All those signs were for *Nina*. Ronnie didn't like me. He didn't like me one bit. He talked to me because of *her*. Everything made sense now. But what had gone wrong? Why did he like her instead of me? When I thought about it, I realized that Nina didn't flirt with him. She didn't encourage him. That would be the ultimate breath sister betrayal. Besides, she liked high school guys better. If anything, she tried to set me up with Ronnie and get him to notice *me*. It wasn't her fault I was too ugly, too dumb, and too unsophisticated to win his heart. So even though I felt extremely jealous of her, I couldn't really feel mad.

I wanted to lock myself in my room and cry, but as I approached the house, I noticed Mom's car in the driveway. How could I hide from her? Every afternoon, she wanted a foot massage and an icy Diet Coke. I had to be her arms and legs, and when I'd finally sit down, she'd ask for a full report about school and then lecture me about finding an interest.

Be brave, I told myself. *Swallow the pain.* I reached in my purse for my glasses, put them on, and stepped through the door.

Instead of lying on the couch and complaining about her aching feet, Mom stood in the middle of the living room with her arms crossed. "Where were you?" she demanded.

Most of the time, I got home first, but even when I didn't, she never acted mad.

"I was at school," I explained. "Study hall. You can call the librarian if you like. She made me sign in."

"Now that's interesting," Mom said. "All of a sudden, you're going to study hall."

"Don't you believe me?"

"Oh, I believe you. You want to know *why* I believe you?"

I was curious, but a little freaked out, too. This was not my normal mother.

"I believe you because I got a phone call," she went on. "From your speech teacher, Mrs. Campos."

"Why did she call? Was it because I couldn't finish my assignment?"

"No, she called because you're not wearing your glasses to class. Apparently, your vision mysteriously improved, but, apparently, not enough for you to see the board."

"I wear my glasses," I protested. "They're on my face, aren't they?"

"Don't sass at me, young lady. After I talked to Mrs. Campos, I called your other teachers, and all of them reported the same thing. So I assume you went to study hall to make up your work?"

Before I could answer, my dad walked in. His eyes were watery, not because he was crying, but because he had contact lenses. Blue contact lenses!

Mom noticed, too. "Don't tell me this is about that job again!" She shook her head and fell onto the couch. "First the clothes, then the hair, and now the eyes? Do you know what kind of message you're sending to our daughter?"

"What's this about a message?" he wanted to know.

"She's not wearing her glasses to school. She probably thinks she looks nerdy."

"I *do* look nerdy," I said.

"You don't want to wear glasses?" Dad asked. "You want some contacts like me?"

"Really? Can I get some?"

"Don't change the subject," Mom warned.

"How did I change it?" Dad said. "We're talking about glasses, right?"

Mom sighed. She was getting very frustrated.

"Look," she said, "every time you change the way you look, you're sending a message to Windy."

"Why?" I interjected. "Because I look like Dad?"

"Of course, sweetheart. You're as beautiful and unique as your dad. You don't have to change a thing, including your glasses."

"It's the truth," Dad said. *"Tu eres muy chula, mija."*

I knew Dad thought I was pretty, but I didn't believe him, or my mom. I understood why he wanted to change himself. For him, the people on TV were the in-crowd. They had light eyes and hair, and they wore the latest styles. Fitting in meant looking like them. The same was true at school. Lots of girls wanted to be breath sisters, so they acted different by playing the choking game. Didn't all the new scarves prove that?

"Windy?" Mom said, because I'd started to cry. I shouldn't have, since I was part of the in-crowd now, but I couldn't help it. Maybe I had breath sisters, but there were other things I didn't have. Like Ronnie. I thought about the time we spent in class, in the cafeteria, in the library, in the hallway, on the school yard. Then I fast-forwarded to this afternoon. And I completely understood how bummed Dad felt when he didn't get picked for the TV job. I felt just as bummed. Didn't I do everything right? Didn't I pay attention to Ronnie, laugh at his jokes, and ask questions to keep the conversation going? Dad was right. He didn't get the job and I didn't get Ronnie because neither of us looked the part.

"I hate my glasses!" I blurted. "I hate my frizzy hair! I hate the shape of my nose and my eyebrows! I hate my fingernails! And if you loved me, Mom, you'd let me fix myself. You'd let Dad fix himself, too!"

I ran to my room and locked the door. Mom followed me and gently knocked.

"Windy, open up. Please. Let's talk about this."

"Go away!" I shouted.

I could feel her waiting patiently in the hallway. Then I heard my dad's steps.

"Mija," he said. "Open the door."

I wouldn't do it. Instead, I got my fluffiest pillow and covered my ears.

After a few more seconds, Mom shouted at Dad. "This is all your fault!"

CHAPTER 13

Gasp

The following morning, Mom knocked at six.

"Windy?" she called, jiggling the locked bedroom door. "Are you awake?"

"I am now," I said sleepily.

"You want to leave early and have breakfast before you see Mrs. Vargas?"

I wanted to sleep another hour, but I couldn't turn her down, because I'd refused to eat the night before. My stomach growled louder than an angry cat and felt as empty as my hopes for Ronnie.

"Okay," I said.

I hurriedly washed up, brushed my hair, and got dressed.

In my rush, I almost forgot to grab the craft book I'd bought for Mrs. Vargas.

I still felt a little upset, so I didn't say much as Mom drove to our favorite breakfast place, the Original Donut Shop on the corner of Babcock and Fredericksburg. It has two drive-thru lanes, one for the donuts and one for the tacos. The taco line is always longer, sometimes with three or four cars idling in the main street. There are two separate lines inside the restaurant, too. On the days we want donuts *and* tacos, we have to stand in line twice. What a hassle! But the food is so good.

We stepped inside. As usual, the air smelled both sugary and *picoso*, the word my family used for the hot, spicy odors of Mexican food. Mom ordered a can of Big Red and a corn tortilla with *barbacoa*, made from the meat of pig cheeks. In my part of Texas, *barbacoa* and Big Red went together like peanut butter and jelly. I wanted my favorite, orange juice and a bean-and-cheese *taquito*. When my *taquito* arrived, I curled the bottom of the tortilla and made a pocket to catch the beans. Otherwise, I'd get my hands dirty. I used to make a huge mess, but not anymore. Eating tacos is a real art.

"The Top Five Traits of a True Taco Expert," I said as I opened my notebook. "Five, ordering potato-and-egg or fajitas on flour tortillas. Four, ordering guacamole and *barbacoa* on corn, always corn. Three, knowing how to bite a crispy taco without cracking the entire shell. Two, folding the ends of soft tacos so the fillings don't drip out. And the number one trait of a true taco expert is?" I suddenly had writer's block. What *was* the number one trait of a true taco expert?

"Never asking for butter," Mom suggested. "Only tourists ask for butter."

I had to agree. The Original Donut Shop didn't even have butter on the condiments table.

"Because tortillas are *not* the same as biscuits or toast," Mom added, as seriously as the principal announcing a warning on the intercom. She made me laugh, and laughing felt good, especially after a whole night of crying into my pillow and asking Raindrop, "Why me?" and "Why *not* me?"

I wrote down the butter comment, put away the notebook, and enjoyed my meal. I was starting to believe I could forget all about Ronnie's crush on Nina, my teacher's phone call, Elena's anger, and Dad's new style. But then Mom said, "We need to talk about last night."

I should have known. Mom and I come to this *taquería* once or twice a week. We always order at the drive-thru, but when she wants to talk, we go inside. This is where she gossiped about her sisters, where she showed me fashion catalogues when she needed an outfit for a dance, and where she explained things like menstruation. Imagine learning *that* while eating tacos.

Mom was silent for a while. I could tell she was searching for the right way to explain things. "Remember that promotion I was offered last year?"

I nodded. In fact, Mom and I had come here, to the Original Donut Shop, to discuss it. Her company had offered to make her a charge nurse with her own office and a big fat raise. I'd thought it was a great idea, especially since she complained about her feet so much, but then I noticed that she said things like, "I'll mostly do paperwork," and "I'll need to go to meetings with the administrators," and "After a while, I'll forget the patients' names." It didn't sound like she wanted the job, so I said, "Mom, do you want to make more money or spend more time with your patients? You know, on your feet. Your tired, sore feet." I wanted her to say, "More money," but she didn't. She decided that she liked standing on her feet all day, and not once has she regretted her choice. She even thanked me for helping her figure it out. But why would she pick sore feet over money? Sometimes adults make no sense.

"Do you know why that decision was so hard for me?" she asked.

I shook my head.

"Because at my age, your father's age, you start to see how far up the career ladder you're going to go." She took a sip of her Big Red before continuing. "They asked me to be a charge nurse, but I said no. They will never ask me again. I'm going to be a floor nurse for the rest of my life. But that's okay, because I chose it. Your father, on the other hand, wasn't offered his dream job, so he didn't have a chance to say yes or no. And the more he thinks about it, the more he remembers his childhood, how hard it was and how he had to prove himself every single day."

"Why did he have to prove himself?" I asked. "Dad's a smart guy. *Everybody* thinks so."

"That's true, *mija*, but when your parents didn't go to college or speak English, accomplishing the American dream is a lot tougher. Maybe that's not *as* true today, but when your father and I were kids, it was the reality."

"Are you talking about people being prejudiced?"

"I guess I am," she said. "It's an ugly subject, but it's history, too. So you can see why your dad is acting this way." She reached over and gently brushed her hand across my cheek. "But, *mija*," she said, so tenderly, "I don't want you to be ashamed of who you are. Maybe the world isn't perfect yet, but it's getting better. I can *feel* it. I can *see* it. You have so many opportunities. That's why I keep bugging you about finding an interest. Think about it. You can be whatever you want to be."

I knew she was talking about my education and career, but all I could think about was my personal life. If Mom was right, then why couldn't I be Ronnie's girlfriend?

"If that's true," I argued, "then why didn't Dad get the TV job? He's good at predicting the weather. He doesn't even need those fancy instruments. He can forecast the whole week after sniffing the air. And every time he and the new guy on TV have a different prediction, Dad's is always right. So you see, Mom, maybe things *haven't* changed."

"I refuse to believe that, Windy."

"Then why? Why didn't he get the job?"

"I don't know." She sighed and crushed her empty soda can. "But we're going to find out in a couple of days."

"How?"

"You'll see."

Soon, I was knocking on Mrs. Vargas's door. When I gave her the crafting book, she smiled and clapped her hands like a winner on *The Price Is Right*. Then she grabbed some Post-its.

"Let's go through the book," she said, "and we can figure out which crafts to make. I'll put Post-its on the ones I really like."

She opened the blinds to the courtyard, and we sat at her table by the sliding door. The book had several sections: for jewelry and hair accessories, for gardens, for wreaths, and for holidays. Mrs. Vargas put most of the Post-its in the gardening section.

"I'm tired of looking at that boring scene," she explained, nodding toward the courtyard. "That fountain used to work, and we used to have herbs, vegetables, and lots of flowers, even the kind that attracted butterflies and hummingbirds. We had an occupational therapist at the time. He used gardening for our therapy. But then he left, and since the next therapist didn't like being outside, we all let the place go."

"Why don't you get together and fix it up again?"

"I guess it seems like too big a project. Where would we start?"

Mrs. Vargas looked out, her eyes full of daydreams.

"It was so pleasant," she remembered. "We'd sit out there, drink our lemonade and enjoy the sun. And even when I didn't go outside, I'd at least have something to look at. But now, even the trees look depressed. Why put all that effort into making leaves if no one's going to enjoy the shade?"

I nodded. The trees did look scraggly.

Mrs. Vargas sighed. "All the crafts in the world aren't going to bring the plants back," she said.

My poor "granny." First the courtyard dried out, and then her friend Mrs. Williams got moved to the third floor. Mrs. Vargas had a lot of worries, just like me.

"Let's make something anyway," I said. "It probably won't help the plants, but at least we can bring in some color. Who knows? Maybe your neighbors will get excited and add their own projects."

We scanned the book again, skipping the birdhouses and feeders because we didn't have a saw, hammer, or nails. Luckily, we found projects we could make — wreaths and macramé holders for hanging baskets. We had one problem, though. We'd have to go shopping first because we didn't have all the supplies.

"I'll ask my mom to take us to Hobby Lobby when she gets off work," I told Mrs. Vargas.

"I'm afraid I can't go today. We'll have to wait for my next check."

Usually, Mrs. Vargas had extra money, but sometimes she spent it. Pleasant Hill has a van, and each week, one of the orderlies drives Mrs. Vargas and her friends to the movies or mall. Sometimes, they see an exhibit at a local museum or walk through the botanical gardens. Other times, they volunteer at elementary schools or help at the polls on election days. Mrs. Vargas likes to stay busy, so she goes on every outing.

"Where did the van go this week?" I asked.

"To El Mercado."

El Mercado is a favorite tourist spot in downtown San Antonio. It has restaurants, *tienditas*, and a museum. *Ballet folklórico* dancers often perform in the plaza.

"Did you have fun?" I asked.

"I didn't go."

"Why not?"

"Because I had forty dollars," she said. "But then it was gone."

"You lost it?"

"Perhaps." She glanced at her dresser as if deciding something. "Perhaps I lost it," she repeated. "Or perhaps someone took it from me."

"You mean it was stolen! Who would do such a thing?" I imagined thugs in ski masks barreling through her door and overturning the mattress, the chairs, and all the dresser drawers till they found her forty bucks — and poor Mrs. Vargas cowering in a corner. I wished I could punch those thieves in the face.

"I wasn't going to mention it," Mrs. Vargas said. "But since it came up, I better tell you about my suspicions."

"Tell me," I insisted. "We can talk to the charge nurse and the security guard. Maybe we can get your money back."

"I don't care about the money, Windy. But I do care about you." She paused a moment, as if deciding again. "I last saw the money a week ago. You come all the time, and you often bring Elena. When you girls leave, everything is in its place. But last week you brought a new friend, and when *she* left, so did my money."

I gasped. "You think *Nina* stole it?"

"Perhaps," Mrs. Vargas said again. "I don't have any proof. Maybe I *did* lose the money. I'm a *viejita* already. Sometimes I forget things."

"You *had* to lose it, Mrs. Vargas. Nina wouldn't steal from you. Why would she do that? She has her own money. And she's really cool, *double* cool. She doesn't have to be my friend, but she *is*. She thinks I'm interesting. I'm her breath sister — which is kind of like the girl version of blood brothers. So you can see how much she cares about me. And because of her, I have a lot of new friends now. Things are better for me lately, a lot better." I couldn't stop myself. I needed to defend Nina. But as I kept talking, I started to wonder. Who was I trying to convince? Mrs. Vargas or myself?

"Okay, okay," Mrs. Vargas interrupted. "I'm just trying to put two and two together. But what do I know? I'm not a detective."

"No, you're not," I said, immediately sorry that I sounded so rude.

I had probably hurt her feelings, but she didn't let on. She dropped the subject after we agreed to shop the following week.

We watched TV for a while, and at noon, we went to lunch. I always eat in the public dining room when I visit Mrs. Vargas. Some of the residents have trouble getting in and out of their chairs, so I become a part-time waitress, bringing them condiments or refilling their tea. I don't mind. I love being near them and hearing their stories. They're the funniest and wisest people I know, and, best of all, they don't have in-crowd or out-crowd sections in their dining room.

"Where were you last week?" they asked. "We thought we saw you in the morning."

"I was here for a little while," I explained. "But then I went shopping with my friend."

Mentioning the shopping trip made me think about that day. Nina had bought lunch, paid for my makeup, and given me cash for the bus, yet at the book fair, she said her mom never gave her money. So why did she have some last

Saturday? Did her mom make an exception, or did Nina take the money from Mrs. Vargas? Oh, no! We had closed our eyes while Elena played the piccolo, and when we opened them, Nina was at the dresser!

The blood must have drained from my face because one of the ladies patted my hand and asked if I was okay.

"Oh, yes," I said. "Just tired, I guess."

And I was tired. Tired of trying to figure people out. Elena never held grudges, but after three days, she was still mad at me. My dad kept changing himself, but instead of being patient, Mom scolded him. Ronnie was super nice now, but he still didn't like me, not the way I liked him. The in-crowd girls were suddenly my friends, but only because I had played the choking game. But what if I hadn't? What if I said I'd never play again? Would they stay my friends? And then Nina. I didn't even know where to start with Nina. She was the most confusing of all.

I was still thinking about all this when I left Pleasant Hill.

"I can't believe I agreed to work two Saturdays in a row," Mom complained as we drove home. "My feet are killing me. I've only had one day off in two weeks. I'm so glad your dad's at Abuelita's. She always sends back food. At least I won't have to cook dinner or do any cleaning. I just want to shower, soak my feet, and watch movies."

She kept talking, but her voice was behind many walls. I kept wondering about Nina. Was she my friend, or not? I considered my TOP FIVE notebook, but this time, I didn't want a record of my doubts. So I mentally made lists instead — all the nice things Nina did against all the times she seemed a little mean. Immediately, the thugs I'd pictured earlier turned into Nina. She didn't have a mask. She didn't make a mess. She wasn't brutal. But, somehow, Nina's way of breaking in seemed worse. She caught me off guard, like a day that started out sunny but then got cold.

"Home at last," Mom said as she pulled the car into the driveway.

We got out of the car and made our way to the porch. Mom unlocked the front door, and when we stepped inside, we gasped. White Poly-fil stuck out of a ripped cushion. Coffee from an overturned cup dripped off the edge of a TV tray. A plant stand had toppled over — the ceramic pot broken, its dirt and ivy leaves littering the ground. Store ads, newspaper pages, and my homework were all over the floor. A confused road of toilet paper crisscrossed the room. And the house stunk. There was definitely poop in here.

"What happened?" Mom cried.

Just then, Raindrop peeked from beneath the couch. He ran to me, rubbed the back of his ears against my leg, and purred like the happiest cat in the world. I'd forgotten to let him out this morning! I must have been too rushed and sleepy. No wonder there was a mess. Even though I didn't witness it, I knew he'd spent the day dashing from room to room, corner to corner, like a rocketing pinball.

"Are you serious?" Mom said. "Another cat, Windy?"

"I can explain."

"Oh, no. Don't bother. I've heard it all before."

"But, Mom . . ."

"Let me guess. He was lonely. He was starving. He needed a home."

She was right. She *had* heard it all before.

"We had an arrangement," she said. "No more cats. Remember?"

I nodded as I picked up Raindrop. He felt so warm and soft. I really loved him and couldn't imagine life without him. A lump formed in my throat, a sign that I was about to cry. I tried to brace myself, but the tears came anyway.

Mom was not moved. "I'm sorry, *mija*, but you have to get rid of that cat. Rules are rules."

"I can't abandon him in the street," I cried. "And if we take him to the shelter, they'll gas him!"

Raindrop jumped out of my arms and scratched at the door.

"Since you decided to make him your responsibility, you'll have to find him a home," Mom said. "Staying here is out of the question. I have to be firm on this. We already have three cats. That's enough. I mean it."

"But I can take care of him, too!"

Mom opened the door, and Raindrop sprinted out. "Look at him," she said. "He's not an indoor kind of cat."

I knew it made no sense, but part of me felt like Raindrop had betrayed me.

Mom headed toward her room. "You have till summer to find him a home. If he's still here by the time school ends, I'm taking him to the shelter, understand?" She turned into the hallway, but before she disappeared behind the wall, she said, "Make sure you clean up that mess."

I could do it. I could sweep the floor, wipe the tables, and try to mend the ripped cushion. I could get this room looking normal again. But what about the other messes in my life? How could I ever clean up those?

CHAPTER 14

Flatliner

W ear your glasses!" Mom said as I left for school on
Monday.

She'd promised to e-mail my teachers to make sure, so I
reluctantly put them on. When I walked into the building,
I was amazed by the details I'd overlooked before — smudges
on the trophy case, faded letters on the bulletin boards, a
missing *F* on the OFFICE sign above the counselor's door.
Our lockers were gray, but where the paint flaked off, I saw
maroon. Some were dented; others, rusted. Mine had a purple squiggle. When did it get there? I saw the coach patrolling
the hall. He wasn't as muscular as I thought — just big and
soft, like the grand prize of a carnival game.

"Hey, Windy!" Liz beckoned me, so I followed her to the courtyard where we found the other in-crowd girls at a picnic table. Everyone talked excitedly about the weekend, but I couldn't pay attention. I was too busy noticing that some of the girls had pimples beneath their makeup. One even wore braces, and another had on glasses, just like me. So why did everyone think they were prettier than the rest of us?

"Look! There's Nina," one of the girls said.

As soon as I saw Nina, my stomach got tight and my foot started tapping the ground — just like each time I gave a speech in Mrs. Campos's class. I inched away, hoping to escape before she reached us, but it was too late.

"Where are you going?" she asked.

"I, um — I, um — you see, I forgot something in my locker."

"Okay. I'll go with you."

"No! I mean, thanks for offering, but I'll only be a minute."

She looked slightly confused.

"Hurry back, then, okay?" she said.

"Sure," I answered.

But I had no intention of rushing back. I hurried down the hall, looking for a place to be alone, to figure things out. I needed to know if Nina stole Mrs. Vargas's money. I couldn't ask her directly, could I? Then again, I couldn't pretend like everything was fine. This mystery had to be solved.

"Trouper, wait up!" Ronnie called.

I turned. As he approached me, I wondered if he had pimples or crooked teeth like I'd seen on the in-crowd girls, but even with my glasses on, Ronnie was supercute.

"Remember what we talked about Friday?" he said.

As if I'd forget!

"So have you talked to Nina?"

"I just got to school," I said, unable to hide my impatience. "What do you want me to do? March up to Nina while she's with her friends, and say, 'Ronnie's got the hots for you!'"

I was mad. I *know* I was mad, but Ronnie didn't hear it. He had a built-in audio mixer, one that muted the sounds he disliked and boosted the ones he favored.

"Good thinking, Trouper. I'm glad you're going to mention it deceitfully."

"You mean 'discreetly'?"

"Yeah. Isn't that what I said?"

"No."

"Sure, it is."

"No, it isn't," I snapped. Then, I did an about-face and walked away.

But there was no way to hide, especially when Nina waited at my locker after each class.

"How was your weekend?" she asked after first period.

I shrugged.

"Did we have any homework for speech?" she asked after second period.

I shrugged again.

After third period, she said, "You're acting weird today. Did something happen when I was absent?"

This time I *did* answer. "You could say that."

"Really? Was it one of the girls? Did somebody say something?"

"No. They were very nice to me," I said.

"Then what? Did Elena act like a brat again? Because it's not your fault she's mad about that silly list."

"It's not Elena."

"Then why are you so moody?" She paused a moment and studied my face. "Is it *me*?"

"You could say that," I repeated. I didn't offer any details. I just took off again.

Nina followed me. She had to, since we were both in Mrs. Campos's class. I went straight to my seat. Elena had already left a piccolo case and lunch box on her desk, but since she wasn't around, Nina pushed them aside and sat down. While I settled into my chair, she absentmindedly bunched one end of her scarf. Today it was a dingy white — like a T-shirt that had been dirtied and washed a dozen times. It had a few snags, too, and a stain near the edge as if it'd been dipped in coffee or tea.

"Talk to me," she said.

I turned away as I reached into my backpack for supplies. Then Ronnie stepped in. He didn't approach us, but he went, "*Psst*," and threw me a thumbs-up.

"What is *that* all about?" Nina asked.

"He likes you," I said. "Not as a friend, but as a *girl*friend."

"Are you serious?"

"Double serious."

She looked at him. He looked at her. Their gazes locked. Only he looked like a gushing puppy, while Nina looked like a bothered cat.

"Alphabetical order!" Mrs. Campos called as the tardy bell rang.

Nina went to her seat in front of Ronnie. Normally, she sat sideways, but today, she gave him her back. He glanced my way and gestured, "What happened?"

Before I could answer, Elena bumped into me because, in addition to the piccolo case and lunch box on her desk, she had her own backpack as well as the presentation board and diorama from last week's book fair.

"Excuse me," she said as she tried to organize her stuff.

"That's okay," I answered. Then, "Did you have a good weekend?"

"It was okay."

I was hoping she'd answer with one of her word-morphs, but at least she said *something*. Mrs. Campos started to lecture, but I couldn't concentrate. In fact, I hadn't been able to concentrate all morning. If I wasn't careful, my C's would slip to D's. I thought about the panoramic pictures in my living room, the lightning, the strong winds. I had lightning and wind inside of me, too, but I wasn't the sky. I couldn't tear through my surroundings whenever I felt like it. So I sat quietly at my desk even though my emotions were a storm.

Finally, the dismissal bell rang. Lunchtime. Normally, this was my favorite part of the day, but right now, I wasn't in the mood for Nina and the in-crowd.

"Are you going to the cafeteria?" I asked Elena.

"No, I'm eating in the band hall today." She strapped on her backpack, tucked her poster beneath her arm, clutched her diorama, piccolo case, and lunch box, and then discovered that she still needed to get her purse.

"Here." I looped the strap around her neck.

"Thanks," she said. She took a few steps toward the exit, but then she turned around. "I'll probably eat in the cafeteria tomorrow, okay?"

I smiled. "That would be coolicious." Maybe the chain latch to Elena's heart was still locked, but at least she'd opened the door as wide as the chain would allow. Maybe tomorrow she'd open it all the way.

I glanced toward Ronnie and Nina's aisle. Ronnie was trying to start a conversation. Nina ignored him, so he gave up and left. I grabbed my things and tried to sneak out, but Nina caught me and grabbed my elbow.

"Come on," she said, leading me toward the restroom. "We need to talk."

Part of me still wanted to hide, but the other part knew I had to talk to her.

Luckily, the restroom was empty. Toilet stalls lined one side of the room, their doors barely connected to the hinges. The walls were covered with patches of gray paint struggling to hide graffiti. One of the windows had a square of plywood instead of glass. A couple of sinks were stopped up with hair or bubble gum, and paper towels littered the floor.

This restroom was a pit compared to the one Nina and I went to at Dillard's.

"I can't believe Ronnie likes me," she began. "No wonder you're so mad."

I placed my books on a shelf above the sink.

"I'm not mad about that," I said.

"Really?" She sat on the window ledge. "That's a relief. I want you to know, Windy — I don't like Ronnie. He's nice, but I just like him as a friend. And I never gave him mixed messages. Especially since *you* like him. I wouldn't steal your boyfriend."

"He's not my boyfriend. Never was."

"I know. But, I wouldn't steal the guy you liked. That's not what breath sisters do."

I saw an opening. "What about money?" I asked. "Do breath sisters steal money?"

"Money?" She shifted her weight on the window ledge. "What are you talking about?"

"Someone took forty dollars from Mrs. Vargas last week — the same amount you had when we went shopping."

She laughed. "You think I took her money since we both had forty bucks? That's just a coincidence, Windy."

"So you *did* have that much?!" I shook my head. Even now, I didn't want to believe she'd steal, but here she was, caught in a lie. "Why?" I asked. "Why would you steal from Mrs. Vargas?"

She didn't answer right away. I could tell she wanted to turn this around, talk her way out of it.

"I didn't," she said. "I can't believe you're blaming me."

"I don't know what else to think. Mrs. Vargas had forty dollars before we visited, but when we left, it was gone. I know *I* didn't steal it, and since you had that much money at the mall . . ."

"You assumed I took it. Is that it? Because Elena was there, too, you know."

"Then at the book fair," I continued, "you said your mother never gave you money."

"I had saved up my allowance!"

She startled me. I'd never heard Nina raise her voice this way. I could tell she didn't like being busted.

"Besides," she went on, "why do you think the money was stolen? Mrs. Vargas is old. She's probably senile or something. She probably used the money to get dentures or whatever old people buy."

Sometimes, when I found myself walking against heavy winds, I had to lean into them and force my way through. Otherwise, I'd be swept away. The same was true now. I had to lean into Nina's lies and force my way through.

"She didn't spend it," I said. "*You* did."

For a long moment, she studied me, but I didn't lower my eyes or step away or take back my words.

"All right," she admitted. "I took the money. But what did I spend it on? Have you thought about that? I wasn't being selfish. I spent it on you, mostly. Can you blame me? You don't know how embarrassing it is — to never have cash — especially when your parents aren't poor. My mom and dad are so into themselves. The only time they notice me is when I'm in trouble, and then they ground me. I'm *always* grounded. That's why I snuck out that day. That's why I took the forty bucks. I just wanted you to like me. Can you blame me for that?"

She started to cry, which made me feel terrible inside. I hated to hurt people's feelings. Then again, why was this *my* fault? I didn't do anything wrong.

Nina wiped her tears with her scarf, and for the second time that day, I saw details I hadn't noticed before — only this time, instead of the hallway, these details were about Nina. I *knew* she didn't feel bad about the money. She felt bad about getting caught. Her words and actions were all lies. If only I could shut them off. First I'd shut off the lie that made me go for Ronnie when I didn't have a chance.

Then the one she wrote about Elena in my TOP FIVE note-book. Then the one that denied stealing money. And finally, the lie about Nina being my friend, my breath sister.

"Can we put this behind us?" she asked. Already, her tears had dried.

Before I could answer, the door opened.

"There you are," Liz said. "I was looking everywhere for you guys."

"We decided to skip lunch today," Nina explained.

"You aren't missing much," Liz said. "They're serving gravy with a little bit of meat and fake mashed potatoes covered in more gravy. It's really gross."

She grabbed a lipstick from her purse and went to the mirror.

"I have to go," I said.

"Stay," Nina insisted.

"Yeah," Liz said. "Besides, it's your turn."

She didn't have to spell it out. I knew exactly what she meant. Last week, I had promised to play the choking game the next time we had a chance.

"She's mad at me," Nina admitted.

"Why? What's going on?"

"It's a long story," Nina answered.

Liz made the "whatever" sign. Then she turned to me. "I'm bummed that you're mad at Nina, but you're not mad at me, are you?"

"No," I said.

She smiled, put her arm around me, and led me to the far end of the restroom. Then, she put her hands on my shoulders. "Are you ready?" she said as she reached toward my neck.

"I, um . . . I, um . . ."

"Don't you want to be my breath sister?" she whispered.

I nodded because I did. I liked having a whole group of friends now — of being included. True, I was angry with Nina, but did that mean I had to be angry with everyone else, too?

So when Liz started to squeeze my neck, I didn't stop her. I closed my eyes and tried to relax, to "go all the way" like they had suggested. They had hinted that it felt good, but once again, a balloon expanded in my head, pushing against my eyeballs and eardrums and tongue. My head felt like a towel being twisted to wring the water out — but instead of water, I was losing my breath. I was going to die — I just knew it. So I tapped Liz's arms. She only squeezed harder. Wasn't she supposed to let go? Wasn't that the rule? "Stop," I tried to say, but nothing came out. I tried

stepping back, but I was against the wall. So I pushed —
I pushed hard. Liz let go and took a few clumsy steps
backward.

"What'd you do that for?" she asked.

I couldn't answer. I needed to catch my breath.

"You don't really want to be a breath sister, do you?"
Nina said.

"It's not that," I managed.

"Then what is it?"

"I just remembered. I've got a book on hold at the library."
Now *I* was a big fat liar, but I didn't care. I just wanted to
get away.

"Don't be such a schoolgirl," Liz teased. "Besides, the
book's not going anywhere."

I lied again. "I need it for a class this afternoon."

Before they could say anything else, I slipped out of the
bathroom and hurried to the library.

I didn't know how I felt or what to do. In some ways, life
at school was better now.

But in other ways, it was worse. As a breath sister, I was
a fake. Nina was already figuring it out, and soon, everyone
else would, too. Then I'd be kicked out of the in-crowd just
like Alicia and Courtney had been kicked out. But even
though I still wanted to be popular, I didn't like the choices

I had to make. I was scared of the choking game, but more importantly, I missed Elena.

I gazed at the books, not really looking at the titles. I just wanted to think. Should I beg Elena for forgiveness? If I did, we'd be friends again. Everything back to status quo. But what would Nina do? Would she turn everyone against me? I'd have out-crowd status for sure, and I'd probably drag Elena down with me. Then, my only hope for romance would be Pimple Jim.

"Can I help you find something?" the librarian asked.

"I'm just browsing."

She nodded and went to help another student. I had no desire to check out a book. *Maybe I should go to a table and study?* I thought. *Wait a minute! Where did I leave my textbooks?* The last place I saw them was in the restroom, on that shelf above the sink. I couldn't believe I'd forgotten them.

I rushed back, pushed open the restroom door, and discovered that Liz and Nina were still in there. But then, I noticed that Nina . . . that she was . . . that she was unconscious on the floor. The filthy restroom floor! Liz crouched beside her, but she didn't seem concerned. Why wasn't she concerned? Nina had collapsed! She looked like a rag doll thrown against the wall. Her legs were bent in backward L's, and her eyes had rolled back, the lids flickering as if she were having a seizure.

I pushed Liz aside.

"Nina. Nina!"

I lifted her chin, tried to rouse her.

"Calm down," Liz said.

"How could you let her pass out like this? So completely? Is this what you do all the time?"

I couldn't think straight. I did fidgety things like straighten Nina's shirt, brush back her hair, and tap her cheek.

Liz said, "Quit freaking out, Windy."

"Do you want her to die?!" I exclaimed.

"That's why we call the game 'flatliner' sometimes."

"Flatliner" made me think of heart monitors, which made me think about the medical shows on TV. They did CPR, right? I'd do it then. I'd breathe into Nina's mouth and pound her chest. I'd get her back. I had to. It wasn't too late.

"Go get the nurse," I told Liz. "I'm going to start CPR."

"Will you calm down? Do you want us to get suspended?"

Just then, Nina's hand twitched. She blinked her eyes.

"Nina?" I said, hopefully.

She took a breath, coughing a bit.

"Nina?"

She mumbled something. I couldn't understand her, but no matter. She was coming back. She'd be okay. She *had* to be.

I grabbed a paper towel, dampened it, and patted her face.

"Say something," I begged.

"Hey." It was only a three-letter word, but Nina managed to make it last as long as a whole sentence.

"Are you okay?"

"More than," she whispered. "More than okay."

She didn't sound like herself. Her words were detached, as if caught in a speech bubble floating away. Her eyes were gradually focusing, though her legs stayed oddly bent. She was the aftermath of a horrible accident that I couldn't help watching.

Finally, she straightened herself and woozily sat up. "That was freaking awesome," she mumbled.

"Awesome?! I thought you were going to die!" I cried. "Why didn't you tap out?"

"Tap out?" Liz laughed. "What's the point of playing, then?"

"What's the point of playing if you're *not* going to tap out?" I argued. "I know you say it makes you feel good, but the game's really about trust, right? It's how you become a breath sister."

Nina reached for my hand. I couldn't believe how cold her fingers were. "You're my breath sister," she whispered. "Both of you are."

Her voice sounded like an old man's. She'd probably messed up her voice box. I glanced at her throat. She wasn't wearing her scarf. For the first time, I got a good look at her neck. Something was definitely wrong with it. A thick horizontal line ran across. Its edges were blunt, and it had overlapping bands of yellow and brown. That was why she always wore a scarf. She didn't want anyone to see the birthmark on her neck. Like her personality, her body had its ugly side, too.

"How can collapsing like a dead person be fun?" I asked Liz.

"*Because.* When the blood rushes back, you get this really cool floaty feeling."

"Yeah, floaty," Nina giggled.

I stood up, disgusted. I didn't have my notebook, but I knew what my next list would be: "The Top Five Stupid Ways to Get High" — smoking pot, drinking beer, shooting up, sniffing glue, and playing the choking game.

"Quit acting like a Goody Two-shoes," Liz said. "It's not like doing drugs. No one's ever been arrested for playing the choking game."

All I could do was shake my head in disbelief.

"Windy," Nina said. "Look at me."

I did. She was getting her voice back, her strength and her wits. I guess the floaty feeling didn't last very long.

"I'm okay, right? And I've done this lots of times."

"Me, too," Liz said.

"See?" Nina continued. "And we're perfectly okay. We're not drug addicts who can't tie their own shoes. And you know why?"

I shook my head again.

"Because the choking game's not dangerous, that's why."

I thought about all the lies Nina had told me today, but this one sounded like the biggest lie of all.

CHAPTER 15

Hyperventilating

*A*fter school, I went straight to my room. I'd had such an upsetting day. The only thing I wanted was some private time with my cats. They were waiting for me. They must have sensed that I really needed them right now. When I put down my things, Cloudy ran to them and stuck his nose in my half-zipped backpack. El Niño purred as he lounged in the sunlight that poured in. And Sunny jumped on a pillow and begged for a belly rub. I didn't have to guess how they felt. Why couldn't people be as easy to read?

I opened the window. "Raindrop!" I called. The bushes rustled when he yawned and arched his back to stretch. "You've been sleeping all day, haven't you?" He sat, licked his paw, and ran it over his head as if fixing a sleek hairdo. I tapped the window ledge and he hopped in. Mom already knew he was here. So why wait till bedtime? He wouldn't get in trouble as long as he stayed in my room.

Cloudy meowed suddenly. One of his claws was stuck in the spiral of my TOP FIVE notebook. "Crazy cat!" I said as I freed him. I shooed him away and then opened the notebook. "The Top Five Cats in the World," I wrote, and even though he died a few years ago, I started with Cyclone. "Five, Cyclone, for being the cat I grew up with. Four, El Niño, for never getting upset or complaining. Three, Cloudy, for being curious about everything — my backpack, closet, shoes, and purse. Two, Sunny, for showing me affection and not caring how I look or what kind of grades I make, or how much money I have, or how cool I am. And the number one cat — Raindrop, for being young and innocent, for not knowing how 'meanormous' people can be."

Poor Raindrop. I had two weeks till summer, two weeks to find him a home. Otherwise, Mom would take him to the pound.

I brainstormed, but I couldn't think of anyone who'd adopt a cat. I had a bunch of boy cousins who'd probably use Raindrop for "experiments" the way they used the gerbils they once had. Elena, even if she were talking to me, had a dog who thought cats were as tasty as Alpo. And there was no way on earth I'd consider Nina after what I saw this afternoon.

I decided to make a CAT NEEDS HOME flyer and post it around the neighborhood or on the announcement board at school. I opened my backpack for some paper and discovered the book I'd bought at the fair, *Careers for Animals*.

"How would you like a job, Raindrop?"

I pulled out the book and flipped through the pages. Dogs had the most career choices. They could guide the blind or assist law enforcers. A bird called a cormorant helped fishermen, while falcons helped hunters. Rats identified landmines, while dolphins found mines in the sea. Horses, oxen, and elephants had jobs, too. But I couldn't find anything for cats. They were probably too stubborn and lazy to work. I was ready to give up, but when I turned one more page, I found it — the perfect job! Research studies had shown that dogs and cats could help people who felt depressed. They were called "pet therapists."

"I don't know where yet, but you're going to be a therapist! You're going to help people, Raindrop."

As soon as I announced my brilliant idea, I heard the front door opening.

"Mom?"

But Dad peeked in my room instead. He was wearing his fancy suit and still had his red hair and blue eyes. He wasn't about to let Mom talk him out of his new look.

"*¿Cómo estás?*" he asked.

"How are you?" was probably the only question I could answer in Spanish. I said, "*Así, así,*" which means "kinda good and kinda bad."

"Is everything okay, *mija*?"

Mom and Dad often told me I could share anything with them. But sometimes, I wanted to work out my problems by myself.

"Tough day at school," I said. "I don't want to talk about it."

Dad studied me for a moment. "If you want to talk later, my door's always open, okay?"

Just then, we heard jingling keys.

"Speaking of open doors," Dad said as Mom entered the house.

"Hello!" she called. "Alfonso? Windy?"

We made our way to the living room.

"Look what I found in the mailbox."

She handed Dad an envelope. He opened it and pulled out a DVD.

"What's this?" he asked.

"It's from the TV station. I called them and told them you wanted to know why you didn't get the job. They said they couldn't discuss it with me, but they promised to send you the audition tape."

I remembered our conversation at the restaurant Saturday when Mom told me we'd discover why Dad didn't get the job. She must have already talked to the people at the station.

"Want to see it?" she asked.

"Of course," Dad said.

He turned on the TV, put the disc in the player, and sat between Mom and me on the couch.

"Finally, you'll understand," he said to Mom. "I didn't look the part back then. But if I went in today, with all these improvements, I'd look perfect."

Mom sighed. "Let's just watch the video." She grabbed the remote and pressed PLAY.

The screen showed the date and my dad's name, while a voice said, "Audition tape for position number 183485." Then the screen showed my dad. Some people gained weight on camera, or the bright lights revealed all their blemishes and wrinkles. But Dad appeared fit and handsome. In fact, he looked *better* than the new guy.

"You look great," I said.

"Yeah," Mom agreed. "You're very debonair on TV — kind of like a Mexican James Bond."

Dad scratched his head. "I do look better than I thought . . . so why didn't I get the job?"

At that moment, a voice on the TV said, "You can begin now, Mr. Soto."

"Now?" my dad asked on the screen. Then he just stopped — like a hypnotized person waiting for a command. A map of Texas with major cities and temperatures was behind him, but he was staring at something right above the camera.

"What were you looking at?" I asked.

"There was a red light on top of the lens," Dad said. "I guess I was looking at that. I didn't realize I was staring at it for so long."

The TV voice said, "Cut!" The screen went black, then the words, "Take Two" appeared. This time, Dad ignored the camera lens. We saw his profile instead. Once again, the voice said, "You may begin now, Mr. Soto."

Dad rushed to fill the silence. "The, um — you know — um . . ." The poor guy couldn't get his words out.

"What happened?" I asked. "Why were you so tongue-tied?"

"Well," he admitted, "I got confused. It doesn't really look that way. On TV, you see a map, but in the studio, there isn't a map, just a big green curtain. You're supposed to look at a monitor to figure out where to point, and at the same time, you're supposed to read words from a teleprompter."

"Mr. Soto," the TV voice said.

My dad turned to it and froze again when he saw the red light above the camera.

"I hate to say this," Mom began, "but you look like a deer caught in headlights."

"That's how I felt. But I was just warming up. In a minute, you'll see me do much better."

On the third take, Dad managed to read the words, but he spoke super fast. I could barely understand him.

"That's when I started to hyperventilate," he explained. "Nerves, I guess. But I get over it. Just wait."

"Take four," the TV voice said.

This time, Dad did better. He avoided the red light above the camera, and he slowed down his words. But even though he was getting through the weather report, he was tapping his foot a lot, and instead of pointing at the map, he was tightening and loosening his fist. He inserted a lot of filler words, too, the same ones I used in speech class —

"okay," "um," "anyway," "you know," and even a Spanish one, "*entonces*." He *never* said "*entonces*" on the radio. Finally, the TV voice said "Cut!" and the audition tape ended.

Next to me, Dad leaned over and stared at the screen in stunned silence. I could tell he felt bummed — double bummed. I scooted closer to him and put my hand on his knee. Mom pressed the OFF button on the remote and then put her arm around him.

After a while, he said, "I thought I did a lot better than that. Especially after I warmed up and caught my breath."

"You weren't that bad," Mom said.

"I was *awful*. I completely choked." He stood up, took off his jacket and tie. "I'm going to the garage. Got some cleaning to do."

"But you'll ruin your new shirt," Mom said.

He just mumbled and walked away.

"Is he mad?" I asked.

"Maybe a little," Mom said. "But at least he knows why he didn't get the job. Your father gets too nervous when he sees the camera."

"That's what happens to me. Every time I have to make a speech, I choke, too. I stand in front of class, and all these people start looking at me. No matter how hard I try, I can't relax. And then I forget stuff, even when I have my notes. It's like my handwriting suddenly becomes a secret code. And then my foot starts tapping like it wants to run off, but the other foot knows better so it doesn't move. It's horrible. It's the most horrible feeling in the world."

Mom patted my shoulder to comfort me. "Everybody has that one class that makes them miserable. For me, it was history. I could never remember all those names and dates."

I smiled. Knowing she had struggled, too, made me feel better.

"Your father's very good on the radio," she went on. "People like his voice and trust his predictions. Maybe it's not glamorous like TV, but the radio's a good job for him. It's where he belongs."

When she mentioned belonging, I dropped my head a little because I remembered everything it took to belong to the in-crowd, to become a breath sister. Playing the choking game and gossiping about others felt wrong, even when I was making fun of my worst enemies, Courtney and Alicia.

"Is something bothering you?" Mom asked.

"I had a fight with Elena," I admitted.

"Because of Nina?"

"Yes. How did you know?"

She shrugged. "Instinct, I guess. Something told me she was trouble."

"Why didn't you warn me?"

"You wouldn't have listened. Besides, you're a smart girl. If Nina was trouble, I knew you'd figure it out on your own."

I didn't think of myself as smart, but Mom seemed convinced. Maybe there were different kinds of intelligence — being book smart like Elena and being smart enough to do the right thing.

Later that night, I opened my TOP FIVE notebook. "The Top Five Things I Learned from My Dad's Audition Tape: Stage fright is genetic; red lights mean stop only when they're hanging above a street; it's better to look like James Bond than Ronald McDonald; not all dreams are meant to come true; and everyone wants a place to belong."

For me, that place had always been the in-crowd, so I started a new list — The Top Five Reasons for Being in the In-Crowd. Then, I stared at the blank page. I stared for a very long time. A month ago, my pen would have scurried across the notebook, but right now, I couldn't think of a single reason to jot down.

*　　*　　*

The next morning, I went to the school's back parking lot and waited for Elena's bus. As soon as I saw her, I snatched her piccolo case.

"I'm holding it hostage till you talk to me."

She didn't even try to grab it back.

"Okay, then, talk."

"I know you hate me right now," I said. "I don't blame you. I deserve it. But I didn't know Nina had finished that list about you, so that's not really my fault except that I should have kept a better eye on my notebook. And I've been a bad friend in other ways, too. I chose Nina over you, and I chose those other girls, too. I admit it. I thought I needed them to be happy. But I already had a friend, one who really cared about me. I can't believe how stupid I've been. I mean really, *really* stupid."

"Yeah," she agreed. "You scored really high on the stupidometer."

I smiled. "Stupidometer? That's a new one."

"What can I say? You inspire me."

"Ouch! That hurts," I teased.

"Then we're even," she said. "So can I have my piccolo back?"

"No. Why don't you give me your gym bag and your tackle box, too?" I reached for them. Then the weirdness dawned on me. "Why do you have a tackle box?"

"Science project," she explained.

She handed me her things, and then we reorganized ourselves to figure out the best way to hold all her stuff. Elena had a shelf in the science lab, a cubbyhole in the band hall, and lockers in the main hallway and in the dressing room. As we toured the school to drop off her supplies, I told her everything. How Nina stole Mrs. Vargas's money. How my dad freaked out at his audition. How my mom found Raindrop. How Ronnie broke my heart. And how the in-crowd played the choking game.

"The what?" she asked.

"The choking game. It's what breath sisters do."

"They choke each other?"

I nodded.

"Why would anyone do that?"

"To get high," I explained. "But I thought it was about trust. At least, that's how Nina sold it to me."

"Trust?" She shook her head. "Let me tell you about trust. Trust is being an ice-skater. Trust is jumping and spinning through the air and knowing your partner is going to catch you. Trust is letting your partner hold you with one hand as he speeds across the rink, and knowing that he's not going to drop you. Trust is keeping people *away* from danger, not *leading* them to it."

"I know," I said, my voice cracking a bit. "I found Nina passed out on the bathroom floor yesterday. I was so scared. But she and Liz thought it was fun."

By now, Elena had a free arm, so she gave me a hug. I felt ashamed but relieved, too. I had jumped in the air, and Elena had caught me.

After a moment, I said, "You really love ice-skating, don't you?"

"Yes. And I love my piccolo, too, so give it back now. I still have to go to the band hall."

I handed it to her. "I wish I had interests like you," I said.

"You *do* have interests. I've told you a million times. You like old people and cats. If you didn't have such a severe case of nerdaphobia, you'd admit it."

"You're really on a roll with the new words this morning."

"Like I said — you inspire me."

I smiled. I didn't care how dorky her words were. I had more fun listening to Elena's silly vocabulary than listening to the in-crowd's gossip. I was going to write a new list, a list of reasons Elena was cool. And the number one reason would be? Word-morphs!

I stopped.

"What's wrong?" Elena asked.

"You're a genius!" I exclaimed. "You're always morphing things — words, ideas, interests."

"Yeah. So what?"

"Old people and cats," I went on. "I like old people and cats, right? Maybe I can morph them together and solve both their problems. Mrs. Vargas has been feeling sad lately, and Raindrop needs a new home. Maybe he can be her pet therapist at Pleasant Hill!"

"What's a pet therapist?"

I didn't answer. I was in the middle of a brainstorm. "If he becomes her pet therapist, I can see him whenever I want, so I'll have *two* reasons to visit the home! My mom wants me to volunteer this summer. I can volunteer at Pleasant Hill! And the first thing I'm going to do is fix the courtyard. That way, Raindrop could have a nice environment, and Mrs. Vargas and her friends could go outside again and enjoy a great view from their windows."

I felt so excited. The morning flew by as I imagined how much fun I'd have working at Pleasant Hill. I couldn't wait to tell Mom. Finally, she could stop bugging me about getting an interest.

I had made up with Elena and found a solution for Raindrop and Mrs. Vargas. The only thing bothering me now was Nina. I couldn't pretend she didn't exist. I had to face her and tell her I couldn't be her breath sister anymore. I got nervous every time I thought about it, but since she was absent again, I had an extra day to work up the courage.

Soon, it was time for fourth period. Mrs. Campos stood at the door, and when she saw me, she called me over. She had a very concerned look on her face.

"Windy," she began, "can you go to the principal's office? I'm excusing you from today's assignment."

"Why do I need to go to the principal?"

"Don't worry. You're not in trouble. He just wants to talk to you."

"About what?"

Mrs. Campos caught a few students eavesdropping and waved them away. Then she whispered, "About Nina."

I swallowed hard. "What about her?"

"I'd better let the principal explain."

I felt as stunned as my dad when he saw that red light above the TV camera. Had Nina been in the principal's office the whole morning? Was that why I hadn't seen her today? Did she get in trouble for something and try to blame me? If she stole Mrs. Vargas's money, then maybe she stole something from the school. No, that couldn't be it. Maybe the principal didn't know about her headaches. Nina was absent a lot. She'd been held back a year for poor attendance. Maybe the principal thought she was skipping school and hoped I could tell him where she went when she wasn't in class. This was the only explanation that made sense, but as soon as I walked into his office, I knew this meeting wasn't about Nina's truancy. The counselor was there, too, and she and the principal looked worried.

They asked me to close the door. Then they pointed to a chair, so I sat down.

"Do you know why you're here?" the principal asked.

"Something about Nina?"

"Yes," he said. "Your teachers say you're her friend. How well do you know her?"

"I met her after Spring Break, about two months ago. So I don't really know her that well."

"But at this school, you know her better than anyone else, right?"

"I guess," I said.

The counselor took off her glasses and leaned toward me. With a real gentle voice, she said, "Windy, did Nina mention any problems she might be having?"

"What kind of problems?" My shaky voice surprised me.

"Problems at home or with kids from her previous campus."

I thought a minute. "She had a lot of friends at her other school. She really misses them."

"And her home life?" the principal asked.

"She was mad at her parents. She said they had grounded her for infinity."

"And she was upset about this?"

"Yes," I said. "I'd be upset, too. Wouldn't you?"

He nodded and scribbled something on a form.

"What's this about?" I asked. "Is Nina in some kind of trouble?"

The counselor glanced at the principal as if asking for his permission. He said, "Go ahead."

"Something happened last night," the counselor began. "It's very hard for me to tell you this, but you are her friend, so you should know." She put her hand on my shoulder. "Last night . . . well, last night . . ."

She couldn't finish her sentence, so the principal finished it for her. "Last night, Nina tried to kill herself."

CHAPTER 16

Suffocation Roulette

The principal and counselor had spoken to a few in-crowd girls, too, so by the time school ended, everyone knew about Nina's "accident."

"Mr. Hamilton got after her for messing up the beat," one of the band kids said. "I guess she felt really bad about it."

"No, she had brain cancer," someone else said. "That's why she got headaches and those bloodshot eyes sometimes. She probably didn't want to go through brain surgery."

Liz added, "I think she had a boyfriend at her other school, and he broke up with her when she got transferred."

And the other in-crowders said, "We knew something was wrong. That's why we got scarves, so she wouldn't feel left out."

206

I couldn't believe all the theories and lies. Nina had never mentioned cancer or a boyfriend. People were making stuff up, and they seemed to enjoy it. Weren't they her friends? Shouldn't they act sad and worried instead of excited by a chance to gossip?

On the way to the bus stop, Elena asked, "Why do *you* think Nina did it?"

I shrugged. "It doesn't make sense. Nina was popular. She was confident. She seemed happy."

"And she *never* messed up the beat in band," Elena added. "She was the best drummer in the school."

We reached the back lot, but Elena's bus hadn't arrived yet.

"Trouper!" I heard.

I turned. Ronnie stood at the gym door and waved me over. I still liked him, but I wasn't going to chase him around anymore.

"You come over here!" I called.

He did, which surprised me.

"Did you hear about Nina?" he asked. "Did you know something was wrong? Why didn't she talk to us? I mean, we're her friends. We could have helped her. Did you tell her how I feel, so she'd know she wasn't alone?"

"Yes."

"But did you make it clear? Because she didn't act like

she knew. She was kind of ignoring me yesterday. Did you say, 'Ronnie likes you,' exactly like that, so she could, like, understand that I care?"

"I said it exactly like that. She knew *exactly* how you felt."

"I don't get it, then," he said. "Why would she hurt herself? She should have talked to me. I could have helped her. I could have been like Romeo, and she could have been Juliet."

"Romeo and Juliet both died in the end," Elena said.

He didn't seem to hear her. He looked truly hurt. *Pobrecito*, my mom would have said — poor guy. I was jealous about the way he cared for Nina, but I felt sorry for him, too.

"Look," I told him. "We can't know how another person *really* feels, even when a bunch of hints are in front of us."

Elena put her hand on my shoulder. She knew how true this was — how I meant it about Nina but also about the crush I had on Ronnie.

He sighed. "Yeah. I guess you're right," he said.

Then he walked back to the gym, hanging his head like a whipped dog.

The next morning, the principal asked the teachers to escort us to the auditorium for an assembly even though the Spring Concert and the Awards Ceremony were scheduled for the last week of school. As far as we knew, nothing else was on the calendar. But we hoped we were in for a treat because the year before, the famous Spurs player, David Robinson, made a surprise visit to give us a pep talk about going to college someday.

As soon as everyone took a seat, the principal stepped onto the stage.

"I'm sure you're all wondering why you're here," he said into the microphone. "As many of you know, we received terrible news about one of our own, Nina Díaz. Last night, we learned some new details. Nina did not try to commit suicide as we first thought." He paused to let this settle in. "She almost died," he continued, "because she was playing the choking game."

I heard murmuring that got louder and louder as my classmates started to talk. Some were saying, "What's the choking game?" and others were saying, "Do you think the principal knows that we play, too? Do you think we'll get suspended?"

"Students," the principal said. "Students!" he said louder. We all got quiet. "I'm sure some of you are familiar with this game," he began. "Maybe you think it's fun. Maybe you think it's safe. But as you can see, it's not. Nina's in the hospital right now. She suffered severe brain damage, and she's never going to be the same. Other kids have suffered brain damage, too, and some have even died. Playing the choking game is as risky and foolish as playing Russian roulette."

I glanced around and caught Liz touching her throat as if to make sure she could still breathe.

"So please give your full attention to Nurse García," the principal said. "She has some important information to share."

Nurse García took the mic from him. As she talked, the teachers passed out brochures about the choking game. I took out my TOP FIVE notebook. I called the new list "The Top Five Choking Game Facts."

1. Nina did not have an ugly birthmark on her neck. She had a ligature mark, which is actually a bruise from the times she choked herself.
2. "Hypoxia" means "no oxygen in the brain." You can have brain damage and seizures even after a few seconds without oxygen.
3. "Asphyxiation" means strangling.
4. "Retinal hemorrhaging" is a fancy way of saying bloodshot eyes. People with bloodshot eyes might be playing the choking game. Headaches and clothes that hide the neck are also warning signs.
5. American dream game, necktie challenge, blackout game, trip to heaven, gasp, flatliner,

hyperventilating, and suffocation roulette are all different ways of saying "choking game."

"The choking game is addictive," the nurse said. "Apparently, Nina played often, even when alone. She was alone two nights ago, and the 'game' went too far. Luckily, her mother found her before she died. But let me make this clear. The doctors say she has permanent brain damage. She will not be able to return to school. She will not be able to play the drums during the Spring Concert or go on field trips or attend the end-of-year dance."

The auditorium was silent. I heard sniffling. Some people wiped teary eyes with the backs of their hands. I gripped the armrest, hoping to keep back my own tears. I knew we were all wondering what Nina was feeling, what she was thinking, or if she could even think at all.

"If you suspect any friends or family members are playing this game, too," Nurse García continued, "please report them. They might be angry at first, but remember, you could be saving a life."

If only I had reported Nina. She would have hated me. I would have been dumped into the out-crowd, for sure. But at least she'd be okay.

CHAPTER 17

Summer

I started volunteering at Pleasant Hill immediately after the school year ended. I didn't want any down time, because whenever I had a quiet moment, I thought about Nina — how guilty I felt for not reporting her and how sad I felt about the way her life had changed. I needed to keep busy. I couldn't help Nina anymore, but I could still help Raindrop, Mrs. Vargas, and her friends.

"Here he is," I said when Mrs. Vargas opened her door.

She peered inside the cat carrier. "He's adorable!"

I unlatched the cage, and Mrs. Vargas reached in. Immediately, Raindrop purred, and when she lifted him to her shoulder, he nuzzled her neck.

"He's so soft," she said, "and so warm and friendly."

"He loves it when you scratch behind his ears."

She did so, and Raindrop purred even louder.

"My goodness," Mrs. Vargas said. "He sounds like a miniature lawn mower." She cradled him as if he were a baby. "I'm glad you talked to the director and got permission to give us your cat."

"I hate making presentations," I admitted. "But Mom said I'd have to convince the director if I wanted Raindrop to be a pet therapist. Luckily, I had to give a persuasive speech in one of my classes, and my teacher made us get statistics and put them on graphs or pie charts. So that's what I did. I got some facts about pet therapy and made a chart. When I showed them to the director, I stuttered and said a whole bunch of filler words, but I managed to get my point across. After my presentation, the director said that bringing Raindrop sounded like a great idea."

"You owe your teacher a thank-you."

"She'll be surprised," I said. "I made C's in her class. I never thought I'd have to make speeches in real life."

Raindrop's whiskers tickled Mrs. Vargas's neck and she smiled. So far, the cat was doing an excellent job. I hadn't seen Mrs. Vargas this happy in a long, long time.

We spent the next hour introducing Raindrop to the residents. I learned that many of them had pets before moving to Pleasant Hill, and they missed having a furry friend to talk to.

"Cats are good listeners," Mrs. Oldman said. "They never interrupt you."

"They make good heaters, too," Mrs. Hernández added. "Nothing like a warm cat on your lap when it's cold."

"Get that thing away from me!" Mr. Rollins said. "I'm allergic."

He was the only one who complained, but since he complained about everything, no one paid attention.

After a while, Raindrop got restless.

"He likes to be outdoors," I explained.

We took him to the courtyard, and he ran straight to the fountain. Then he started sniffing around.

"He's going to love it here," I said, "especially after I fix it up."

That's what I had volunteered to do — fix and maintain the courtyard. I got a roll of trash bags, gardening gloves, a bucket of soapy water, a rake, and a broom. First, I cleaned the benches. I dipped a rag into the soapy water and scrubbed. I couldn't believe how much dirt had collected on the seats. I spent over an hour cleaning them. Because it was sunny, the benches dried quickly, and soon, some residents came to sit outside. One even brought a pitcher of icy lemonade, the perfect treat. After the benches, I decided to rake and sweep the dead leaves. Mr. Rollins came outdoors and said, "It's about time someone cleaned up this mess!" Then, he grabbed an extra broom and started to help. I felt grateful even though he kept saying, "Haven't you ever raked a yard before?" and "Pick up the pace. I've got bad knees, but what's your excuse?"

Every now and then, Raindrop pawed at my shoes, wanting to play. I'd shake him off. At one point, he looked at me, his giant blue eyes full of questions.

"I've got work to do. We'll play later."

Just then, one of the ladies called, "Here, kitty, kitty!" She dangled a bell tied to a string. Raindrop sprinted over and pounced on it. The lady swung the bell higher and higher. He jumped for it, then pretended to stalk it. The residents laughed at his antics. This was his first day as an official pet therapist, and he was already a pro.

After scrubbing the benches and spending the entire afternoon with the rake and broom, all I could do when I got home was plop on the couch and take off my shoes. I leaned back, closed my eyes, and enjoyed the air-conditioning. Mom disappeared to her bedroom, so the house was peaceful and quiet. I would have fallen asleep, but Dad walked in.

"How was your first day as a volunteer?" he asked.

"Perfect, but I'm really tired."

He nodded. "Like mother, like daughter," he said.

I noticed he wasn't as dressed up as usual. "Where's your coat and tie, Dad?"

"I didn't wear a coat today. Too hot. And I must have left my tie at work. It got a bit stuffy in the office, so I took it off."

Just then, Mom stepped into the room with the VibraSpa. She filled it with hot water and turned it on.

"Put your feet in there," she said.

I did and immediately felt soothed by the water and soft vibrations.

"This feels great!" I said.

"Now do you see why I love my job? Even when it makes me really tired?"

I *completely* understood. Helping others was hard work. Some, like Mr. Rollins, were always in a bad mood, but others were grateful and kind. Spending the day on my feet was exhausting, but at least I accomplished something. The courtyard benches were clean and the dead leaves had been cleared out. These small improvements delighted the residents. Seeing them happy made *me* happy. Who cared if I felt tired? Working at Pleasant Hill was a lot more fun than sitting at a desk all day.

I thought about my future. I didn't want to be a nurse like Mom, but maybe I could look into different kinds of therapy jobs, especially those for old people.

"Can you think of five types of therapy jobs?" I asked Mom.

She paused a moment, then counted with her fingers as she said, "Physical therapy, speech therapy, occupational therapy, respiratory therapy, and massage therapy."

"Why do you ask?" Dad wanted to know.

"It's for a new list — a list of possible careers."

They smiled. They didn't say anything, but I could tell they were happy to learn that I had finally discovered an interest.

Elena went to band camp during the first month of summer. I didn't see her often, but we talked or texted nearly every day. When band camp ended, I took a break from Pleasant Hill, so Elena and I could spend the day together.

After my dad dropped us off at the mall, Elena said, "Your dad's hair isn't red anymore."

"He's letting it grow out," I explained. "He's not wearing blue contacts, either. Or suits. He says the hair coloring, contact lenses, and suits aren't worth the trouble."

"Is he still bummed about that TV job?"

"No. In fact, he *loves* being on the radio now. Remember those rainstorms a couple of weeks ago?"

Elena nodded.

"When the power went out, no one could watch TV. So they took out their radios, and guess who they listened to?"

"Your dad?"

"Yes! He worked overtime that week, giving frequent weather updates and news about road closures. Now he gets a lot of fan mail."

"That's great!"

"It really is," I agreed. "It's nice to see Dad happy again, but it's weird, too."

"Why?"

"Because his life hasn't changed. He's right back where he was a year ago. Only now, he likes it."

"Well," Elena said, "sometimes you have to try new things to appreciate what you already have."

That was so true. Like how hanging out with the in-crowd girls last spring made me learn that Elena was the best friend I could ever wish for.

We reached the main corridor of the mall where salespeople tried to lure us to their kiosks with promises of free samples.

"No, thank you. No, thank you," we kept saying.

Once we got to a quiet place, I asked, "What do you want to do first?"

"I've been saving my allowance for three months," Elena said, "and since I made straight A's, my parents gave me some bonus money. So I'm treating you to lunch, and then we're going to every department store till I find a nice bathing suit and sunglasses."

"That's going to take all day."

"I know, but at least we won't get bored. Besides, walking around the mall is good exercise."

As it turned out, we didn't walk around very much. We ordered Subway sandwiches at the food court, found a table, and spent the next few hours catching up.

I told her all about the courtyard at Pleasant Hill. "We put in plants that attract butterflies," I explained. "And in one corner, we're making a cactus garden. We've got three bird feeders, too. Now that the fountain is running, there are a lot of birds."

"Does Raindrop hunt them?"

"Not really. He stalks and charges, but so far, he's been too slow to catch them. He'd rather take naps and sunbathe. Mrs. Vargas calls him *flojo*."

"'*Flojo*'?"

"It means 'lazy.' "

Elena laughed. Then she shared pictures from band camp. One face kept popping up.

"Okay," I had to ask. "Who is that cute guy? And why do you have a hundred pictures of him?"

"I don't have a hundred pictures. Only eighteen."

"You counted?"

"I couldn't help it. I'm a hopeless guy-mantic."

"Guy-mantic?"

"Romantic about guys," she explained. "I've got a serious case of Mark-mania right now."

"Is that his name? Mark?"

She nodded, then giggled, then told me how he's the drum major at Irving Middle School, how he's been texting her every day.

"And on the last day of band camp, he gave me this." Elena reached into her purse and pulled out a bookmark. Two teddy bears held hands, and in the heart that floated above their heads, it said, "Love is forever."

"Do you think it means something?" she asked.

"It *totally* means something," I said.

She smiled. I could tell she had a serious crush on Mark, but before she could say more, I felt a tap on my shoulder. It was Ronnie. "Hi, Trouper. Good to see you."

He still had the cutest smile. Normally, my heart raced when I saw it, but today, I felt a bit annoyed.

"Don't call me Trouper," I said. "It makes me feel like a Boy Scout."

Ronnie laughed. "I didn't know girls could join Boy Scouts."

"They can't."

"Then why do you feel like one?"

"Because you're always calling me Trouper."

He stared at me, the blankest expression on his face.

"Troops," Elena tried to explain. "Boy Scouts have troops."

"I know," he said. Then he turned to me. "But you're not a Boy Scout. I mean, 'cause you're a girl, right?"

I sighed. Had he always been this dense?

"Forget it," I said. "Forget about the Boy Scouts. Just don't call me Trouper anymore. My name's Windy. So call me Windy."

"Sure thing, Tr . . . I mean, Windy."

He punched my shoulder in a playful way, and I punched him back. Then he took a seat to visit us for a while. Normally, the idea of sitting at the mall with Ronnie would be a dream come true, but now it didn't feel like a big deal. I still cared about him, but he didn't make me boy crazy anymore. I'd been too busy these past few weeks to think about him, and now that I saw him again, I couldn't find those feelings I once had. They had disappeared as surely as a puddle on a sunny day.

After a while, a shadow fell over the table. I looked up. Ronnie's uncle. He had a bag from GNC, a store that sold vitamins and protein shakes.

"Ready?" he asked Ronnie.

"Sure thing," Ronnie said. "See you girls later."

We waved good-bye as he walked off. When he was out of earshot, I said, "That man is Ronnie's uncle, his idol. I used to think I couldn't live without Ronnie, but I don't feel boycentric about him anymore. He's still cute, but all he talks about is going to the gym."

"You're just figuring that out *now*?" Elena said, and then she cracked up. I should have felt offended, but I had to admit that I'd been a bit blind about Ronnie. He was nice and cute, but dense. A boyfriend, I decided, should be someone you could talk to, *really* talk to.

After we had a good laugh, Elena said, "Let's hurry. My mom's coming in an hour, and I still need to find a bathing suit."

We walked toward Dillard's, but we didn't get too far before running into Courtney and Alicia. A whole pack of in-crowd girls followed them. I couldn't believe it. They were leaders again, which meant life at school would be miserable next year. Courtney and Alicia didn't have their usual headbands, and none of the girls wore scarves. Apparently, the new dress code for popular girls called for big, jangly bracelets.

Once again, Courtney and Alicia cornered Elena and me.

"Hey, noose-heads," they said.

"Excuse me?" I sassed back.

"You're a noose-head because of Nina and the choking game."

"Yeah, I get the reference," I said. "But for your information, I was never into that."

"That's not what *we* heard." They nodded toward Liz, who stood behind them. As soon as she caught my glance, she turned away.

"You know what else we heard?" Courtney asked.

"I don't really care," I said.

She was determined to tell me anyway. "We heard that Nina slobbers all over herself. She's got to wear a beach towel as a bib."

They all laughed. They thought it was so funny. I knew they were mean, but this was outright cruel. Then again, picking on someone who couldn't defend herself was easy, and Courtney and Alicia liked easy targets. When someone challenged them, they backed away. Didn't that happen when Nina stood up for Elena and me the very first day we met her?

Remembering this, I took a step forward and got in Courtney's face. "So what if Nina slobbers?"

"Yeah, so what?" Elena echoed.

"At least it's not as ugly as the trash that comes out of *your* mouth," I said.

Courtney stepped back. She looked a little scared, but she quickly got over it. "Whatever," she said, flashing the *W* sign, this time with the light jingle of her bracelets. "Come on, girls." She marched off, Alicia, Liz, and the others following like obedient ducks.

"Some things never change," Elena said.

I nodded. "I'm not going to let Courtney and Alicia get to me anymore," I said. "They've always been mean. But Liz upsets me. She pretended to be my friend last year. She pretended to be Nina's friend, too. She played the choking game, and she went a lot further than I ever did. I can't believe she's laughing about it now. What a hypocrite."

When I said that, Elena looked at her feet.

"What's wrong?" I asked.

"Maybe we're hypocrites, too."

"What do you mean?"

She shrugged. "Nina's accident happened two months ago. We haven't seen her. We haven't called to see how she's doing. We didn't even send a get-well card."

She was right. We'd spent the summer pretending like Nina didn't exist, but even though we hadn't known her very long, she had left traces of herself behind — Raindrop's collar, the lists we wrote at the mall, her drum riffs, her advice about boys, the way she stood up to bullies. These were the positive details, but Nina had her dark side, too. After all, she stole Mrs. Vargas's money and sabotaged my friendship with Elena — not to mention bringing the choking game to our school.

"I really liked Nina," I admitted. "I thought she was cool. But I got mad at her, too. If she hadn't been hurt, if she were here today, I don't think I'd be her friend."

Elena nodded. Then we made our way to Dillard's. We shopped in silence. There was plenty to discuss, but somehow we knew that talking about something else meant turning our backs on the topic of Nina — something our hearts no longer wanted to do.

CHAPTER 18

Breath Sisters

*T*he first time Elena and I called Nina's house, her mother cried.

"You don't know how much this means to us," Mrs. Díaz said. "Nina used to have so many friends. She used to be so popular. But no one calls her anymore. No one visits. My poor baby's all alone."

We heard her sobbing, and we felt guilty because we'd avoided Nina, too.

"Is it okay if we come by and spend time with her?" I asked.

"Oh, please do. Nina needs to see people her own age. I know it would cheer her up."

There was a long silence. Elena and I had questions about Nina's condition, but we didn't know how to ask. Mrs. Díaz must have understood because she said, "Nina's not the same person anymore. She might not remember you. She . . . she . . ." We heard a few sniffles. "She can't do a lot of things, and when she tries, she gets frustrated. Sometimes, she gets . . . combative."

"We know she's changed," Elena said.

"It's still shocking when you first see her. So I'll understand . . . if you don't want to come after all."

Elena and I looked at each other. This was our last chance to decide whether to accept or turn away from Nina. But we had already discussed it, and we knew what we wanted to do.

So that's how we spend our weekends now. One Saturday, we see Mrs. Vargas and Raindrop, and the next Saturday, we see Nina. Mrs. Díaz was right. Nina is not the same person. The first time we saw her, we had to fight back tears. We think she remembers us, but sometimes we're not sure.

There are many things Nina can't do, but she can walk if she holds the wall. She can throw a ball, though she can't catch one. She can slip her legs through a pair of jeans and her arms through a shirt, and she can close a zipper if she concentrates really hard. But forget shoelaces, buttons, and the tiny straps and buckles on her sandals. They get her fingers all tied up. Forget, too, the drums she used to play. She hits her own legs by accident or drops the sticks. Forget text messages because she can't remember her letters. Forget board games, card games, or video games. She can't understand the rules or hold the pieces.

Nina can say "no" clearly, even though her tongue gets stuck on the *n* sometimes. She can say "yes," but only if she holds the *s* till her breath runs out. Anything longer than one syllable turns into a stream of consonants, no vowels in between. Sometimes she forgets to open her mouth when she speaks, so her words sound like noises trapped in a cocoon. I don't understand her. I hate when I don't understand her because I know she has something important to say.

I wish Nina and I still shared classes, but she doesn't go to school anymore. She rides a bus to a center. Instead of teachers, she has tutors and learning specialists. Instead of a P.E. coach, she has an occupational therapist.

Nina can laugh and blush when you tell her she's pretty. But she doesn't hold a pencil right, and when she tries to spell her name, a long squiggle ruins the page. Her mother tucks a paper towel into her collar like a bib because sometimes Nina's spoon veers to the left before reaching her mouth. And if we try to help her, like the time I wiped some ice cream that had dribbled onto her chin, she'll push me. She'll push real hard. I'll fall back and bruise my hip against the counter. Then Mrs. Díaz will apologize over and over again because she wants me to come back. She doesn't want Nina to lose her only friends.

I know it's weird to spend time with a person who pushes me when she's upset — who throws a book, a glass, whatever's handy when she gets mad. Who acts like she hates me sometimes. Often, Elena and I *force* ourselves to visit Nina's house. We'd rather starch and iron my dad's whole closet of clothes or pull weeds or do homework. We can think of better ways to spend our Saturday afternoons, but we go to Nina's house every other week. We don't even discuss it. We just go.

We go because one day, Elena had brought her ice-skating DVD and put it into the player. It featured highlights from the previous Olympics. We couldn't tell if Nina was watching because sometimes her eyes looked off to the sides of things. But she must have been paying attention. One skater completed a perfect triple axel. He looked so beautiful and free as he twirled in the air. When he landed, we clapped with delight, and Nina said, "Mmmaa . . . mmma . . ."

She couldn't finish her word, and I worried that she'd

throw something because of her frustration. But then, Elena said, "That's right, Nina. That was a mag-tastic jump!"

Nina smiled because that was exactly what she'd tried to say, but also, I wanted to believe, because she knew that Elena and I understood her. Like an ice-skater, she didn't need sentences or words to tell us how she felt.

She clapped again and we joined her. Then Elena and I put our arms around Nina. We all held each other for a long time, and that's when I realized what being a breath sister truly meant.

Dear Readers,

When three of my middle school students arrived to class with bloodshot eyes, I thought they were high on marijuana, but I was wrong. They had done something that was much more disturbing. They had played the choking game, and what worried me the most was their belief that it was harmless fun.

I soon learned that the choking game was not unique to the students at my school. In fact, many young people around the country had already died or suffered brain injuries while playing this "game," and like most people who hear sad news, I wanted to know why. Why do people play the choking game? Why do young people, especially, do *anything* that is risky or dangerous? I also wanted to know what it's like to be the person who gets hurt or the person who stands by and lets it happen.

This is what makes books so special. They allow us to live through someone else and learn through their mistakes. That way, we don't have to fall into the same traps. I hope this book is the only experience you have with the choking game and that Windy and Nina's story is enough to discourage you from taking part. But, if you are playing, please stop, and if you aren't but know someone who is, please be a good friend by reporting them.

Sincerely yours,

Diana López

DANGEROUS BEHAVIORS WEBSITE
http://thedbfoundation.com
The Dangerous Behaviors website offers statistics, testimonials,
warning signs, parental advice, medical information,
and awareness about the choking game.

CHOKING GAME AWARENESS BLOG
http://chokinggameawareness.blogspot.com
This blog/discussion board was established to raise awareness
and educate parents, children, and educators about the
dangers of the choking game.

G.A.S.P. WEBSITE
http://www.stop-the-choking-game.com/en/home.asp
The G.A.S.P. website (Games Adolescents Shouldn't Play)
provides testimonials, statistics, and a support forum for families
who have been affected by the choking game.

Acknowledgments

My deep appreciation goes to Amanda Maciel at Scholastic and Stefanie Von Borstel at Full Circle Literary. I'd also like to thank those who read drafts and gave me insightful suggestions — Connie Hsu, Irma Ned Bailey, Cindy Leal Massey, Linda Schuler, Bill Stephens, and Florence Weinberg. Thanks to Mom, Dad, Albert, Tricia, Steven, and my beautiful nephews and nieces who show so much love. Also, for much-needed moral support and for listening to my ramblings about the ups and downs of the writing life, my heartfelt gratitude goes to Vanesa Sanabria, Caryl Paulsen, Christine Granados, Kirk Woller, Rick Nichols, San Juan San Miguel, Ken Esten Cooke, and my dear friend and mentor, Dagoberto Gilb. And, always, always, thank you, Gene.